Will Thomas is a New Zealander based in Sydney who loves sport, wine and crime fiction. A capable sportsman in his youth, Will played first grade cricket and rugby and has completed a marathon, a half Ironman and a dozen half marathons.

After a career in the wine business, this is first novel.

To Helen – Faith, Gorgeous

Will Thomas

THE CHAIRMAN

AUSTIN MACAULEY PUBLISHERS™

LONDON * CAMBRIDGE * NEW YORK * SHARJAH

A CIP catalogue record for this title is available from the British Library.

ISBN 9781398410640 (Paperback)
ISBN 9781398410657 (ePub e-book)

www.austinmacauley.com

First Published 2022
Austin Macauley Publishers Ltd®
1 Canada Square
Canary Wharf
London
E14 5AA

To the Collective Fiction – thanks CC and the group

1

Spirited applause was not unusual at Eden Gardens. Test matches brought crowds that were enthusiastic and parochial in equal measure, so the fall of a wicket inevitably brought celebration. The applause this morning was in response to the dismissal of Harish Lal, the Indian opener, after a brief but volatile innings. Eight boundaries in the first ten overs of a Test match were a thrilling spectacle and the crowd acknowledged the audacity of Lal's play, particularly as it came against the generational enemy from across the border, Pakistan.

The applause didn't signal delight at Lal's dismissal but it heralded the arrival of Pradip Mistry, a player whose esteem in India gave even the cows a run for their money. Around the world, his quality as a cricketer was acknowledged without hesitation and barely a Test match passed where he didn't evoke deletions and new entries into the record book.

Not wanting to fly in the face of public opinion, Mistry concurred that he was in fact pretty special and often pondered on how remarkable it was that such a good sportsman could also be so incredibly good-looking. His bearing conveyed a sense of divine privilege, a demeanour that seldom endeared him to those that breached his inner circle. Not, surprisingly, he was on very few speed dials among his opponents and they worked assiduously to ensure he would not re-write records against them. They were seldom successful.

Mistry sat in the dressing room, immaculately kitted and apparently ready to begin another matchless onslaught. His hair was gelled down, his collar up and his green eyes seemed to be rehearsing the thousand-yard stare he reserved for the unworthy.

The crowd knew that Mistry liked to make them wait to make an entrance. This time, though, the legend was overdoing it and the crowd began to chant in a seductive rhythm, urging him to appear. For their part, the Pakistanis began discussing an appeal for timed-out.

Mistry's captain, Srinivas Srinath, was moved to check on Mistry, so he hurried down the stairs to the Indian room. As he entered, he could see that Mistry was ready to bat – pads strapped on, gloves in the helmet – and leaning back in his chair as if barely willing to design such a tawdry attack.

Then Srinivas Srinath realised why the crowd had to wait. Although, to all intents and purposes, his star batsman was ready, there was one severely limiting factor – the large shard of mirror buried into the side of his neck. The dressing room mirror had been shattered and the red carpet, that Mistry had insisted on, camouflaged the litres of blood that had flowed from his carotid artery.

The skipper knew immediately that it was game over at Eden Gardens – and game over for Pradip Mistry.

2

Mike Dunn loved Sundays. The combination of a beer buzz, a suite of newspapers and the prospect of a fry-up of industrial proportions gave the morning a sort of muddling serenity. Others chose a walk in the woods for their Sunday morning reverie and he could see their point, but for him the angry sputter of a middle rasher left the blackbird's warble a sorry second.

Dunn also saw Sundays as a day of reflection – not on the deeper quandaries of humanity but on the previous day's sport. In the winter, it was the satisfaction of watching his beloved Harlequins, a rugby team he had watched as a boy, played for as a young man and now enjoyed with a pint and some old mates. Come spring, he took the field for his village cricket team, the Old Ecumenians. Dunn loved the frothy exuberance of the dressing room as much as the cricket – his day job didn't typically allow for a great deal of humour, so the banter and bonding were both his relaxation and his release. Dunn had been a competitive sportsman in his day and still bore the muscular frame of an athlete but also bore the outcomes of many a Saturday afternoon collision.

Dunn woke late and was moving gingerly as he stooped to pick up the stack of Sunday papers sitting at his front door. The sight of Pradip Mistry on the front page was unusual and at first Dunn thought he must have gone past Lara's Test record or had found another way to fall foul of Fleet Street. The headline 'Murder Mistry' was as bewildering as it was annoying for as a detective for the International Cricket Council, Dunn was caught between astonishment at this apparent crime and piqued that a Sunday paper should be the bearer of the news. His mobile phone was often on silent during the weekend and as he scrolled through, he could see there were messages from many parts of the world and several from his boss, the increasingly irritated Guy Trinnick, chief investigator of the ICC. The first of his four messages began cordially enough as he conveyed the news of Mistry's death. The last was distinctly cool.

Mike, you and I are booked on the four o'clock flight to Kolkata. I'll see you at the airport.

He looked down at his phone and checked his now aborted plans for the day. So much for the Sunday session at the Ring of Bells.

3

Thank God we're up the front of this plane, Dunn thought as the flight entered its ninth hour. He'd spent an hour poring through the details of the crime and its scene but found photos and the printed word were no replacements for experiencing the scene and absorbing its feel. In his experience, every scene had a tone or an ambience that a camera just couldn't catch. After a post prandial cognac, he'd exhausted the movie selection and although he found a few albums he liked in the music offering, he felt that listening to *Beast of Burden* at full noise for the tenth time could ruin the song for good.

Guy Trinnick had proved to be ordinary company, which didn't surprise Dunn given their relative backgrounds and dispositions. He couldn't believe Trinnick had chosen to travel in a navy-blue pinstripe suit, white shirt and a club tie of some persuasion and felt a bit under dressed in his ink-coloured slim fit jeans, a sky-blue V-neck merino top and his favourite indigo jacket with purple lining.

Dunn was a casual man in a serious job – Trinnick was a serious man who seemed to play everything with a straight bat. Whether it was matters cricket, law or his weekend passion of philately, Trinnick was not a man with whom flippancy or inattention to detail sat well. Everything had its place and its purpose and anything beyond this structure was imbued with risk. He was happy to eat and drink but being merry was never quite on the agenda. Trinnick was also an ambitious man with his sights set on a desk at ICC headquarters in Dubai. Solving crimes and a squeaky-clean personal life would see him there before his 60th birthday.

In the course of their working lives, many had been the time that Trinnick had censured Dunn for his Machiavellian approach to process and what he considered needless sparring with the press. In the same breath, Trinnick knew that, maverick that he was, Dunn had a terrific track record of solution with many forms of match fixing, bribery of umpires and pitch tampering, all but removed from the game. 'All but' being an important distinction with corruption never far away from a game that was a bookmaker's heaven. Trinnick was smart enough to realise that although they may not sit down and discuss the latest valuation of the Penny Black or watch football with a few pints of bitter on board, his partnership with Dunn was a successful one. Although he would only admit it if he was held down and had a blowtorch bearing down on him, Trinnick knew that he needed Dunn. Getting to the truth on the demise of Pradip Mistry was going to need Dunn's remarkable nose for crime.

4

Dunn's instinct for wrongdoing was fashioned early in his life – at about the same time his loathing of privilege began to manifest. Surprisingly, both traits were developed at public school, an odd English term, which suggests they are open to all when in fact 'public' schools were about as open to the general public as the back bar at Raffles. At thousands of pounds per term, they were typically the domain of the wealthy.

Dunn, whose father drove a taxi and whose mother worked in the office at the local comprehensive, was able to attend only because of 80-hour weeks from his father and his mother's extraordinary frugality. Unlike many of his peers, his first day was the start of secondary school and as he climbed from the family sedan, the rotor blades of a helicopter buffeted his farewell embrace. It proceeded to set down at about deep square leg on the main cricket oval, sending autumn leaves off on a dervish dance and the Head Groundsman into a fit of pique. From within, a slight young man with undeserved swagger emerged, closely followed by enough luggage to clothe an entire dormitory. It was Dunn's first glance at Piers Vasher and his first impression of 'complete cock' remained resolutely undiminished in the years that followed.

Vasher was of the view that since 'Daddy' had paid for the cricket nets to be resurfaced (and, to prove that mobile phone entrepreneurs possessed an appreciation of culture, had financed the new acoustics in the auditorium), he should bat three, field at first slip and wear the number ten jersey on the rugby field. Dunn, as an elegant and at times muscular batsmen and an industrious loose forward, took the view that Vasher might like to front at the trials like everyone else. Apprising Vasher of this opinion meant the chance of a friendly coffee and a cheese roll in the dining hall together went from unlikely to inconceivable in as long as it took to say, "I don't care if your old man makes the Queen look a bit short of a quid, the master in charge picks the team."

Although spot on in principle, the relevant master returned for the Christmas term sporting a tan that didn't result from lounging in a deck chair on the Blackpool pier Were one to speculate, Barbados or The Bahamas would have seemed the likely provider of the sunshine and the greeting he gave Vasher would suggest that Vasher's father was the likely provider of the holiday.

The school years that followed elicited an uneasy co-existence and although both played in the same sporting teams (eventually making the 1st XV and 1st XI), 'teammates' applied only on the team sheet. In their final year, Vasher, who was already earmarked for a spot in Daddy's firm, decided that making a bit of cash on the side was a better bet than worrying about exams or other trivia. Apart from the inherent benefit of having a bit of extra folding, it meant he could confidently navigate the occasional expenditure audit that his old man put him through. Having to create a plausible reason for buying 200 pounds worth of stationery, which was actually 50 quids worth of stationery and 150 on a dead cert at Fontwell Park, was never pleasant and his father made him sweat through every flaky reconciliation.

Convincing youthful and, at times, admiring pupils that his racing syndicate was a great way to bolster their funds for the summer holidays was easy. For five pounds a week, Piers would run through the fields with his dad's bookmaker and apparently place educated bets on behalf of the syndicate. There was of course a small management fee and he'd be happy to take one off bets from anyone who thought they'd spotted something interesting beyond the syndicate's wagers. Subscribers were not difficult to find, particularly when convinced by Vasher's resident bully boys, Matt Grose and Fraser Boyle, that being part of the syndicate was a significantly better option than having their cigarettes taken or their food lockers eviscerated.

After a couple of early wins, word got around that this was the greatest money-making venture since the Aga Khan pieced his strategy together. Vasher was light on detail but would distribute news of the week's balance through nominated runners in each house. As long as the balance was heading north, his punters were happy and as many of the group had been press-ganged and found horse racing as interesting as floral arrangements, there was little enquiry into method.

Little enquiry, that was, until Mike Dunn became interested. After Ben Varcoe, one of his junior housemates, filled him in on the deal, Dunn sensed heartache ahead for the constituents of the racing syndicate. As they predominantly hailed from the junior ranks and Vasher was leaving school forever come July, Dunn sensed a rort of the Ponzi persuasion. Using Varcoe as his eyes, Dunn followed the performance for a few weeks, seeing nothing untoward in a moderately increasing tally. Maybe the old man's bookie was guiding the punt well or maybe he was going each way on favourites and keeping ahead on place money – but, unfortunately, there was nothing about Vasher's demeanour that suggested a big divvy up come the end of term and a few celebratory pints at The White Swan.

Because the information on performance was of a general nature and all that came back was a running balance, Dunn wanted to find out when and where the bets were being placed. He called Varcoe aside.

"Ben, I want to get Vasher to place a bet for me. Ten pounds on Velvet Lightning in the fifth race at Epsom."

"Ten pounds, Velvet Lightning. I'll catch up with him after evening lessons tonight."

That Friday afternoon, Dunn saw Vasher and his ever-present cronies, Grose and Boyle, head out of the main gates and down toward the direction of the local village. Following at a plausible distance, he watched the three of them enter the local William Hill and made his way to a conveniently placed lamp post, where he leaned nonchalantly waiting for the trio to reappear.

Vasher was first out the door and gave Dunn the sort of look reserved for one who has broken wind in private only to find his girlfriend's mother had entered the room in stealth.

"Dunn, fancy seeing you here!" He imparted with exaggerated bonhomie.

"Vasher, the pleasure's mine. Look, I'm just checking on a bet I got one of the boys to put on with you. Horse called Velvet Lightning."

"Oh, was that you? Bit of a roughie, Dunn, no joy there, I'm afraid. Sorry to be the bearer of bad news."

"Thanks, Vasher, I appreciate that but there's just one thing. There is no Velvet Lightning." Vasher's eyes narrowed in the manner of a rookie gambler whose bluff has been called.

"That's right, Vasher – I knew something was up. Nothing rang true about this whole caper, so I thought a little dummy run might bring a few things to light. So tell me, if you're not placing all the bets you're asked to, how does the whole thing work?"

By now, Boyle and Grose had made their way out of the shop and were providing just enough menace to make Dunn wary.

"As you're not a member of the syndicate, I'd say that how it works is none of your fucking business." Spat Vasher. "I'm helping some kids make a bit of pocket money, so why don't you just sod off?"

"I'd be happy to Piers but I don't like seeing people get parted from their cash unfairly, most of whom have only joined up because of pressure from these two scrotes."

"Be that as it may, no one has complained and in fact the balance is increasing. The fact that it might all go on an all or nothing during the last week of term is just the way racing works old son. Bring on another Velvet Lightning, I say."

"Well, 'old Son', here's how this bit of racing is going to work. You're going to distribute all the funds tomorrow according to the last update you gave. Thank everyone for taking part and pop in a five-pound bonus to show what a good bloke you are."

Grose had heard enough and thought the best way to dissuade Dunn was throwing a big haymaker in his direction. This was an error in two parts – the speed of his punch was such that he might as well have sent a text message to tell him it was on its way and his lumbering technique meant he had no guard to speak of should Dunn respond in kind – which he did. Grose was not used to being struck as he was usually only up for violence against those much younger or smaller. Dunn was neither and as boxing formed a part of his training regime, a straight right, delivered at an open target, was spreading Grose's nose from the left of his top lip to the base of his right eye at about the same time that he realised his haymaker hadn't quite found the target.

Boyle observed this and although he could faintly hear Vasher urging him to 'Smash him', his primary instinct was self-preservation and although he knew it would mean the end of freebies and nights in the Vasher family's corporate box at White Hart Lane, he suggested to Vasher that Dunn was right and they should return the money straight away.

"All right, Dunn – you win. For now. How about we keep this chat to ourselves, yeah?"

"You make good with the money and I don't see why not Piers."

With that, he turned and strolled back up the lane to school, feeling good about exposing Vasher's fraud but a little remorseful about damaging Grose so badly – mind you, nothing like putting a bully in his place. He would be wary of Vasher and the end of term couldn't come quickly enough.

5

Trinnick and Dunn were driven to Eden Gardens directly from the airport. Trinnick feeling fresh after total abstinence and large quantities of mineral water. Dunn feeling just a tad dusty after making his way through numerous selections from the wine list in the final hours of the flight. What began as an attempt to induce some sleep soon transformed into an urgent search for a drinking companion. As it happened, luck was on his side. Two rows back and equally insomniac, he'd found Alpa Parekh, a post-graduate student from Cambridge, returning home to Kolkata for the holidays. Alpa, as Dunn described to an utterly disinterested Trinnick, was the image of the girl in *Bend it Like Beckham*, except older, he hastened to add. Trinnick's only response was a bemused look and a request for focus.

On reflection, Dunn couldn't quite decide whether she was amused by him or simply enjoyed the distraction but her willingness to provide her phone number left him encouraged and looking forward to reacquainting at some stage. That is, if he was going to be able to find time with the workaholic Trinnick as his shadow.

"Mike, we're here. Get your mind to join us and let's get on with it," snapped Trinnick, all too aware that his call for focus had gone unheeded.

They made their way down to the dressing room, escorted by an extremely courteous member of the BCCI. His name was Bharat Patel and he was the point person for all matters on the death of Pradip Mistry.

"Good morning, Mr Patel. Tell me who has had access to the crime scene?"

Patel raised his palms as if Trinnick's question had been an accusation and his response indicated why. "No one, apart from the Indian captain, who is deeply distressed, the Kolkata police representatives and perhaps one or two players."

"Is that all?" replied Dunn with more than a whiff of sarcasm.

"Well…I did bring my wife in for a look too," replied Patel. "It is a momentous occasion in the history of Indian cricket." He began by way of protest but Dunn knew that, as crime scenes went, this one was about as contaminated as the public baths in Chernobyl.

"Mike, forensically, this is a cot-case. What we've got to establish is how the hell someone got in here and what made them drive a piece of mirror into his neck."

Although tempted to reply, "Yeah, thanks, Sherlock." Dunn knew that Trinnick was right. There would be no point calling in the crime-scene scientists on this one.

"Mr Patel, who could get access to the dressing room during the Test?" inquired Trinnick.

"Well, only the players can get past security but, of course, for a few rupees or the promise of a favour or two, it is amazing how distracted the guards can get. Fans would pay big money to meet with Pradip Mistry in private, if you understand my meaning."

Crikey, thought Dunn, thinking back to the photos of Mistry's body. He didn't know who was screening his talent but any woman who could bury a piece of mirror that far in would need arms like a commando.

"Mr Dunn, do not get me wrong, male fans would come through as well, buying souvenirs and selling them on Amazon or eBay – it is a thriving business, this memorabilia."

Dunn knew he was approaching needle-in-a-haystack territory – corrupt guards meant pretty much unfettered access for the right sum of money and it sounded like men and women alike frequented the inner sanctum at Eden Gardens.

As they entered the dressing room, Dunn scanned the interior looking for exit and entry points and anything that looked incongruous. The usual debris of a cricket dressing room presented itself with gear bags, bats, tracksuits and protective equipment strewn around the room. Had he not been a cricketer he may have assumed signs of a struggle but this was situation normal for most rooms he'd seen. A blood stain which had turned a red earth hue made a perimeter around the area where Mistry had sat for the last time. A lanyard which had once been around someone's neck sat crumpled beside the outline of the body.

"Let's find out who was wearing this." Dunn said as he bagged the item and handed it to Patel. "Although everyone in the bloody ground seems to have one these days. Let's see if we can rule a few people out at least. Mr Patel, can you get the Chief of Police to have the guards brought in for questioning?"

"I will do that and I will also arrange for the guards to be brought in for questioning myself. I don't need the help of the chief of police to bring the guards in and I'm yet to be convinced I need you either, Mr Dunn," said Mr Patel. "I will see you back here at 9 am tomorrow."

"All right, Bharat. Let's work together on this, shall we?" They strolled in silence back to the main foyer and shook hands in departure with only a nod.

Dunn's mind wandered as they returned to the hotel and as they disembarked, he rummaged in his pocket for the boarding pass where Alpa Parekh's details were held.

6

Sydney is frequently written up as one of the world's great cities. From Conde Naste to Lonely Planet, travel writers have expended all manner of superlatives describing the New South Wales capital. Sydney is the city for all comers – 50-dollar mains meet fish and chips in the park, million dollar launches cruise by the Manly ferry and at the Sydney Cricket Ground, corporate boxes hosting seven-figure executives share the ground with families in the bleachers. Whether sipping chilled champagne in elevated luxury or soaking up a Tooheys New or six at the base of the Brewongle, Sydney crowds agreed that watching Mitch Howard bat for a session was worth the price of a season ticket, let alone the admission for the day's play.

This ground had its share of favourites over the years – Bradman and Ponsford, Walters and the Waughs had all thrilled the crowds of their era but there was something about Howard that magnetised a crowd. Most of the world's greats tended to be known for a certain style-elegance or abrasiveness, technical perfection or innovation but few had ever displayed the prism of styles that Mitch Howard had at his command. Regardless of the situation or the quality of the attack, Mitch Howard played with a certainty and an imperviousness that even his detractors had to acknowledge with tight-lipped praise.

And, yes, great player that he was, Howard had his detractors. It was not that Howard was often outwardly rude or obnoxious, it was just his obsession with perfection left others a little cold. Mitchell Howard was concerned with scoring the most runs at the fastest rate in the history of Australian cricket. He had no room for anything else in his life but beating the runs that Ricky Ponting had accumulated over 287 visits to the crease. Selectors and administrators were dealt with perfunctorily. He never expressed it directly but his manner suggested well enough that regardless of his unwillingness to attend sponsor's functions, drink at the members' bar or give interviews, he knew he was first name on the sheet.

Such behaviour was annoying for many but there was general acceptance of his quirks as the requirements of a champion. Not surprisingly, Howard was a fanatical trainer, and once his teammates had had enough, he would have the net bowlers bowl until their arms were horizontal. The last person to make eye contact was ordered to set up the bowling machine, where the finishing touches were applied to his preparation.

It was Thursday afternoon and the players were preparing for the season ahead, which included a busy calendar of Test matches, ODIs and T20s. This summer's opponents were New Zealand, followed by a series against a resurgent West Indies. Mitch loved playing the Kiwis and even though Cam Peters had touched him up a couple of times early in his career, matches against New Zealand had provided a good chunk of his international aggregate.

Net practice was over and as the rest of the team headed for the showers, Mitch picked up his kit and headed for the indoor nets. One of the net bowlers had got under his skin and, perfectionist that he was, Howard wanted to spend another half-hour or so feeling the leather pinging from the middle of his 2lb 12 oz. Gray Nicolls, as a young man, he had dreamt of being sponsored by a gear company and he loved the striking logo and clean willows that Gray Nicolls produced. Although not short of offers, Howard still got a kick out of going to the factory and picking up half a dozen bats made exactly to his specifications. They were big pieces of willow but beautifully balanced and more than a few times, teammates had swapped the stickers from their sponsors so they could use one of Howard's blades.

The killer watched as Mitch Howard made his way to the indoor net facility. He had arranged a membership for the gym at Moore Park, which made access to the facilities remarkably simple.

Howard had been working hard and, as was his want, was getting ready to put in those vital extra minutes that separated the great from the good. It was getting late and helpers to feed the bowling machine were getting hard to come by but the killer's attire of an NSW Blues fan shirt and navy tracksuit pants didn't raise eyebrows or warrant a call to security. Howard just wanted someone to feed the bowling machine – if they could put a ball in a chute, they were good enough for him. A young boy approached the killer and asked if he could help with practice.

"Hi, kid. Look, we're trying a few new things tonight. I think Mitch would prefer a private session."

"But, sir, I've been here all day. I was told I could feed him a few balls if I stuck around to the end."

"That's a shame, Son. They've given you a bum steer there. I'm afraid it's a no for tonight."

The sight of tears welling might have induced flexibility in some but the killer had long ago eschewed emotion and sentimentality and remained resolutely dry-eyed. He also knew that the last thing he needed was a helicopter parent visiting the nets and complaining about how little Tobias should be given a turn on the machine. Peeling off a couple of crisp green hundred-dollar notes, he gestured to the boy.

"Sorry, it didn't work out today. Since you're such a good sport, go and get yourself some new gear or something."

The money made the lump in little Toby's throat disappear and he scuttled back to the car park with a couple of hundy in his pocket and the prospect of being home in time for an episode of Sponge Bob.

The killer set up the machine and waited for Howard to appear. He heard him before he saw him.

"New balls, mate – and crank it up to 150ks," he barked as he entered the nets.

The killer observed his quarry. Pads, protector and thigh pad in place, Howard ambled down to take guard and prepare for the session. Wearing his one-day international pants and a tight sponsor's T-shirt, he looked the epitome of an international cricketer. His fit frame and muscular arms in stark contrast to the muffin-topped players of yesteryear.

Not wanting to raise any concerns, the killer made sure the first couple of deliveries pitched nicely, just short of a length, allowing Howard to stroke them into where the cover field would be. The new balls danced a bit off the seam but Howard was able to get in line and leave or play accordingly.

After the first 36 deliveries, Mitch leant down and picked up one of the balls, which moments before had been the recipient of a particularly violent late cut. Whipping of his helmet, he began to gather the rest of the balls down his end.

156 grams of polished leather, six seams sitting proudly, a new Kookaburra cricket ball was the colour of a good pinot noir and harder than the practice wickets at the WACA.

The killer watched Howard as he bent to pick up a ball, made a subtle adjustment to the machine and watched as one of the new 'cherries' whirred past

Howard's ear. Howard's response was predictable and a tirade of abuse flowed down the pitch. The killer raised the direction of the machine a few degrees and fired the next ball at his throat, turning a well-practiced expletive into an onomatopoeic gasp. Howard reeled and tried to steady, momentarily fixing his eyes on his assailant. The killer caught the register in Howard's eyes. "Hello, Mitchell – been awhile…"

There was to be no further opportunity for re-acquaintance. The next ball struck Mitch Howard on the right temple and the killer realised that he had achieved something few other bowlers in the world had – he had beaten Mitchell Howard's defence and with a noise like a golfer using a three-iron on a ripened peach, he had confirmed Mitchell Howard's mortality.

7

Checking in at the Hyatt in Kolkata, Trinnick and Dunn were stunned by the obvious opulence, situated not two blocks from desperate poverty. The palm-tree-lined drive and ornate water feature created a distinct barrier from the rest of the city. Dunn had heard such stories from cricketers returning from tours but neither the wealth nor the destitution had been done justice. The lobby was all polished granite and shiny smiles, as an army of staff made a good fist of anticipating one's every requirement.

Handing them their keys with a gesture of practiced welcome, the receptionist pointed to the lifts and motioned to the bell boy with an exaggerated flourish of her uniformed arms.

"I wish you well in solving Pradip's murder, gentlemen," leaving neither in any doubt as to their lack of anonymity.

Dunn threw his bag on the side table, sat on the bed and unlaced his shoes. Loakes were perfect for London but in India, they doubled as a slow cooker for his feet, which ached and throbbed in painful rhythm. An ice-cold Cobra or two and the sleep of the dead was the extent of Dunn's agenda but he knew that a hotel meeting room, Trinnick, and a run-through of the day's notes was pretty much a certainty.

Dunn waited for Trinnick to call but the thought of a hot shower and a lather up was irresistible. Inevitably, the phone rang just as the temperature became perfect, which elicited a nude dash and an ungainly sprawl across the bed to grab his phone.

"Mike, Guy here. I've booked the Topaz room – it's a little large but it's all I could get at short notice. Have a shower and let's meet in 20 minutes."

"Good shout, sir. Perhaps we could organise a couple of beers and some of that Bhuja mix?"

"Perhaps. See you in 20 minutes – and bring your notes too if you would."

Well, thought Dunn, I wasn't expecting gin and tonics in the lobby bar but ice water and a hotel meeting room seems a bit bleak.

The bathroom was now impenetrably steamed and Dunn enjoyed washing 12 hours in the air and eight on the ground from his body. He dressed, threw on a splash of fragrance and made his way to the lifts.

Trinnick's predictability delivered once more with pages of notes and a bowl of mints the only adornment to the meeting room table.

"Seriously, Guy, can't we do this with a beer and something to eat?"

"Mike, a beer is on its way. Let's look at this for an hour and call it a night. We'll summarise what we know and get a good night's sleep. I don't see tomorrow getting any easier."

"OK," said Dunn. "First impressions – Mistry, a prize git if ever there was one, is taken out as he waits to bat. Likelihood of the killer doing so unnoticed – close to zero. So, motive unclear but means and opportunity suggest assistance – a person or persons has been paid to look the other way."

"Agreed," Trinnick responded. "But the killer would have only needed seconds to walk in and commit the murder."

"Yes, 15–20 seconds and Mistry is off to the land of flat tracks and dribbly mediums."

"Mike, please, be respectful. I'm not keen on your rather unfortunate brand of humour causing an incident over here. Prize git or not, Mistry had legions of admirers in this part of the world and we're going to need every scrap of goodwill if we're going to progress this inquiry."

Dunn leant back on his chair and considered a witty rejoinder but Trinnick's face convinced him this would be a foolish move.

"Sorry, just a little jaded. I'll be diplomacy personified with the locals. Now, apart from Bhagwat Puttaswamy and his troop of guards, who else have we got on the list tomorrow?"

"Let's work through ground staff, dressing room attendants, the team manager and a few of the players. And let's not forget Mistry's family."

"Sounds good. Tell me, is Abhishek Misra among the players we still need to talk to?"

"Yes, half the team were up in the stand and have been identified by CCTV but we need to confirm where Abhi and the rest of the players were at the time of the murder. I've arranged for those players not on CCTV and the support staff to come in and have a chat."

"I know Abhi from a while back. We played a few games of cricket together when he was a youngster – super bloke." Dunn recalled the elegant young man who had joined his team at late notice and stunned everyone with his exquisite talent.

"Great. Might be a good opportunity to build some rapport. I'm sure not everyone is thrilled to have a couple of Englishmen investigating what at the moment could be viewed as a matter for local law enforcement."

"Yes, I'm sure Abhi will be onside. He's very influential because of his background and his incredible record for India."

"All right, let's put a plan together for tomorrow."

As they shuffled papers and typed up a schedule, Dunn's beer arrived as crisp and delightful as only a long-awaited lager can be.

Dunn motioned to the waiter. "I might get you to grab another of those, thank you."

Trinnick sent him a disdainful squint. "Mike, you haven't even had a sip!"

"I know, but by the time he's made it to the bar and back, this one will be long gone." Dunn grinned and raised his glass while Trinnick shook his head slowly and continued typing.

"OK, Mike, let's talk to Misra together and then you take the guards and I'll take the rest of the players."

Dunn drained his beer and nodded. "OK. Looking at the dressing room, there's no way anyone gets in without going through that door. Which means someone got careless or someone was encouraged to do so. I'm sure motivation will reveal itself at some stage tomorrow. The guards have to hold the key, pardon the pun."

As Dunn's second beer arrived, Trinnick snapped his laptop shut and gathered his things. "Righto, Mike, enjoy your beer. See you for breakfast at 7."

Dunn raised his glass. "See you then, sir, cheers."

8

Dunn was relieved when his head finally hit the assortment of pillows at the head of his bed. Upon returning from the debrief with Trinnick, he'd made the fatal error of assessing the quality of the mini bar, then compounding it by flicking on the television and seeing if he could navigate the remotes and catch up with sports results from home. Half an hour and a miniature of Johnnie Black later, he was none the wiser and giving serious thought to the Belvedere.

Unusually, Dunn made the better choice, setting his alarm for 6.30 am and looking forward to a full night's sleep. He woke to an unfeasibly dark room for what he was sure was the morning, only to discover that he had slept for an hour and had the rest of the night ahead of him.

This, like many other nights before, was not a good time for Dunn.

Mike Dunn had begun his working life as a policeman. His talent for investigation and natural leadership style was spotted early and before long, Dunn was running a small squad of detectives that were placed on specific task force activity, their role to shut down waves of crime that would surge in from time to time as new demographics brought with them methods and ventures unfamiliar to UK policing. It had been work which involved considerable danger – Russian people smugglers not being familiar with 'fair play' – but with success came profile and Dunn's prowess was acknowledged as something that other investigative bodies might find useful. Cricket was having major issues with corruption, so Dunn was brought across to assist, initially in an advisory role.

A competent cricketer with a detailed knowledge of the game, Dunn understood that although cricket enjoyed its share of unlikely results and outcomes, there were certain things that just didn't ring true. Off spinners bowling a no-ball in the 11th over of a spell, batsmen charging down the pitch when nicely settled on the first morning of a game – it was clear there was something afoot and that bookmakers were making markets on events other than the outcome of the game. This practice, known as 'spot fixing', was much harder to determine than match fixing because it was easy for one player to influence the result. To fix a match in a team sport like cricket, many people would have to be involved but bets on an individual's actions were much harder to detect. A bowler conceding more than ten runs in the first over of the match could just be the result of a poor start and some good batting rather than a deliberate attempt to deliver a result for a bookie sitting in front of a laptop in another country.

Dunn's initial work drew a few blanks, as every anomalous piece of cricket began to engender suspicion. Honest cricketers after a brain fade were being questioned and it appeared the investigative team were operating more by guesswork than deduction. It was time to start using data more wisely by creating some links between the players and the incidence of oddities to provide an investigative path.

Dunn's data whiz was an unlikely character for the role, a giant Old Etonian, with a bank account at Coutts and Co. and a career in the army behind him. Jolian Ford-Robertson didn't take kindly to people besmirching the good name of cricket and, fortunately, had an almost savant like ability in pattern recognition. He appeared at the office ready for work in a pale blue cotton button down and ivory chinos from Hackett along with a pair of Churches brogues, every inch the former public schoolboy.

"Good morning, sir, how are you?" he intoned with cheerful enthusiasm. "Really chuffed to be on board again."

"Pleased to have you back, Jolian. I have to say data searches aren't really my thing."

"No trouble, sir. I think I can help you with that. I've had a look at the files and I've come up with a plan to get us underway."

"Well, that's great news, Jolian. So, how do you think you'll turn all that information into something useable?"

"Quite simple, really, sir. We'll just have a look at the data of every cricket match played at first-class level or above for the past 12 months and cross reference a data set created from all performances, three standard deviations or more from the average. Shouldn't take long."

"Thanks, Jolian. Sounds like an extremely solid approach," responded a slightly confused but utterly relieved Dunn. He wasn't completely au fait with the mathematics but he did realise that Ford-Robertson was going to turn a complex wodge of data into what he hoped would provide some workable leads.

"Tell you what, you get going on that and I'll head down to Lord's. There are a couple of guys playing in the county match there that I'm keen to chat to. Let's compare notes tomorrow morning."

"Excellent, sir. Should be done by then," replied Ford-Robertson, already tapping in queries on multiple screens.

Dunn left knowing with complete certainty that it would indeed be done, even if it meant Ford-Robertson would work through the night. Once he got started, only food, cigarettes and coffee would divert him from his task.

Dunn strolled down to the underground and got the next train to St Johns Wood, making the short walk to the Grace Gates just as the Middlesex team were taking the field. He'd hedged his bets well as he wanted to chat to Middlesex opener Simon Westbrooke or Somerset's Australian fast bowler, Harry Dalton. True to fast bowler form, he soon found Dalton in shorts and a Mambo T-shirt, enjoying a cup of tea at the back of the dressing room as his batsmen gathered their kit and made their way onto the balcony.

Dunn had considered it a minor miracle even getting to Dalton, making his way through the plethora of white-coated officials who took their roles extremely seriously.

"Harry, my name is Mike Dunn. I'm working for the ICC and was wondering if I could have a word."

Dalton looked up from his phone screen. "Yeah, mate, no worries. D'ya wanna talk here or maybe we could nip down to the dining room – might need another brew anyway."

"Sure, Harry, that sounds good. I'd love a cup of tea myself."

They made their way downstairs and took a seat at one of the long tables. Dunn forwent small talk and gave Dalton a quick summary of the situation.

"Harry, the reason I want to talk to you is that you play in a number of competitions – Test and One Day cricket, IPL, BBL back in Australia – you're involved in all of them. I'm investigating match or spot fixing and I need to find out what you know. Anything you've heard, suspicious behaviour, anything that might help us get to the heart of this."

"Sure, Mike, I see where you're coming from, mind you, it's a bit hard in T20. There's weird shit going on all the time. I haven't seen or heard anything within the Australian dressing room – only the occasional strange bit of fielding from the opposition but nothing you'd pin anyone on. Reckon, I could mis-field too when we're 360 for three on a 35-degree day at Adelaide Oval."

"Yes, good point," replied Dunn. "Actually, Harry, it's the T20 stuff I'm most interested in. It's where the money is but it also brings together a whole bunch of players from around the world. What a brilliant opportunity to build a network."

"Yeah, too right. As you may know, I play for Hyderabad. Good bunch of boys – couple of Kiwis, a Pom and then mainly Indians. We're a pretty tight group but there's one guy who is always lurking around dressing rooms, chatting to young guys in the team whenever we play them. Always goes out of his way to be friendly – even came up and shook my hand and told me how much he loved my game and it was only five minutes after I'd given him a massive spray. He plays for Pakistan, been going for about a year. Name's Faisal Shaikh."

"Well, Harry, that's been really helpful. Enjoy your season over here – and all the best for the Ashes."

"Ha! I know you don't really mean the last bit but thanks. And I'll keep an eye out. Can't have these wankers ruining our game. Any of the other boys you want to chat to?"

"No, but thanks. I'll have a chat to Simon Westbrooke in the break."

"Gee, don't get in between him and the buffet – could be dangerous!" He laughed loudly and headed back upstairs. Dunn refreshed his tea and wrote up his discussion, pleased to finally have a name to work with.

Dalton's knowledge of Westbrooke's fondness for food was accurate, as Dunn's approach for a chat was met with a "Sure but let me grab some sandwiches first – had to do a bit of running out there". Westbrooke was a burly young man in every respect, his arms chunky but not cut and his trousers doing all they could to justify the makers claims of stretch in the fibre. He made his cricket living by hitting very hard, very often, which meant the odious prospect of running between the wickets was not one he had to contemplate too frequently. T20 was a game made in heaven for the likes of Westbrooke and county cricket was a necessary evil and an ideal way to keep his hand in.

"Sorry," said Westbrooke as he sat down. "Missed your name back there – a little preoccupied with lunch."

"No problem. The name's Mike Dunn and I work for the ICC. Was hoping to have a chat about some corruption issues the game is facing. We're particularly interested in anyone who has played in the IPL, mainly because of the big web of international players involved in the competition. We feel there are players intimately involved with the bookies and we're going to find them."

"OK, I'm happy to help," he replied as a blob of butter from an asparagus roll nestled on his chin. "What exactly are you after though? Not sure what I can tell you."

"I'm interested in players who are recruiting. We know there are minnows doing their bidding but it's the link back to the bookies that we need to solve."

Westbrooke's sleeveless sweater was now scattered with crumbs from a variety of sandwiches and an unfortunate dollop of sauce that had slid from his party pie.

"I'll give that some thought but there's no one who really stands out in that regard. The only guy that I find a little curious is Angelo Da Silva – he seems to find ways to do 'stupid things'." Westbrooke's fingers made air quotes as if to suggest there was nothing random about them at all.

"OK, well, look, if there is anyone else who springs to mind, give me a shout. All the best."

"Thanks, Mike, you too. Would be nice to think everyone was trying."

Dunn strolled down to Baker Street station and decided to finish his day off back at home. No need to invade Ford-Robertson in full data crunch. It was time to do some research on Da Silva and Shaikh.

9

As he entered the office the following morning, a smell combining the worst of Lambert and Butler King Size and meat lover's pizza confirmed that Ford-Robertson had indeed put in a monster shift in order to get the data sorted. As a big man, his body odour seemed to fill the space like an overweight passenger in economy class and Dunn suggested they nip out for coffee to do the debrief. Not surprisingly, Ford-Robertson took tea to Dunn's latte and they settled into conversation.

"Well, sir," Ford-Robertson began. "It took me awhile to get the data sets appropriately ordered and then I had to run a few dummy variables to make sure I would arrive at something conclusive. There's often a danger of multi co-linearity in this type of brief. I have to say that the exercise in looking for unusual performances was not especially rewarding. Very little that on second examination couldn't be put down to the quirks of the game – human error if you will. I was feeling a little despondent at about a quarter to two this morning, so I decide on a different angle. Instead of focusing on the performers of unusual acts, I thought about broadening the focus, drilling up, as it were, and seeing if there was a regular face or two that were playing in matches with incidences of unusual performance if not directly involved themselves."

Dunn knew that amid those sentences, Ford-Robertson was on to something and rather than interrupt the flow simply motioned with his eyebrows and a nod of the head that carrying on would be perfectly acceptable.

"Well, sir," he began again, "with all the players around the world appearing many times away from their home countries and often playing with other players. There is significantly higher opportunity to forge relations that previously wouldn't have existed. When I cross tabbed the unusual performances with the players from both teams, one name kept coming up."

"Excellent work, Jolian. What name was that?"

"The Pakistani opener – Faisal Shaikh."

Dunn headed for lunch, feeling exhilarated. Ford-Robertson's search provided nothing more than circumstantial evidence but given progress to date, it felt like placing Colonel Mustard in the study. Phone calls to other players mid-morning had confirmed that Shaikh had indeed had conversations with a few of them, conversations that treaded cagily around the subject but suggested that there was money to be made if they wanted to talk further. Dunn knew that he needed someone to testify and was reminded of Westbrooke's remarks about Angelo Da Silva. He knew that Da Silva was contracted to Sussex for the English summer, so it looked like a trip south was in order.

Dunn negotiated his way out of London and dialled a number he'd got from the receptionist at Sussex County Cricket Club.

"Angelo speaking."

"Hi, Angelo. It's Mike Dunn here. I'm an investigator for the ICC and was hoping to have a chat with you."

"What about? I don't think I can help you." His tone was unusually wary and Dunn's senses heightened.

"Hang on, Angelo. Let me tell you what it is about first. Why don't we meet in Hove tonight and I can let you know what we are looking into?"

"I've got training tonight, sorry."

"Angelo, I've just driven past Gatwick and I'm not turning around. I'm happy to wait until after training. How does 8 pm at The Robin Hood sound?"

"Well, I'll try, but I can't promise anything."

"OK, Angelo, I'll see you there."

As soon as the phone clicked off, Dunn hit the phone button on his steering wheel to report in. The call went straight to voice mail so Dunn obeyed the prompts and left a quick message. "Good news, sir. We've managed to connect some dots and I'm heading down to Sussex to talk with Angelo Da Silva. We're meeting at eight o'clock tonight, so I'll check back in the morning. Bye."

Traffic was light for the rest of the journey and it was little after six when Dunn checked into the Hilton. He caught the lift to his 9th floor room and enjoyed a long shower and a packet of Pringles from the mini bar. At ten to eight, he made the short walk along Kings Road and then turned right on to Western Street toward The Robin Hood. He ordered a pint and took a seat at the back of the pub, hoping that their conversation could be as discreet as possible. The pub was busy but not heaving and two people having a conversation over a pint was unlikely to attract any attention, nor have a lonely drinker suggest a drink together. At half past eight, a young man in tracksuit pants and a Sussex team sweatshirt entered nervously and scanned the bar. There was a fidgety nervousness about him and Dunn nodded and beckoned him over.

"Angelo, how are you?" Dunn stood and offered a hand which Da Silva took with obvious reluctance.

"I'm fine but I'm not sure I have anything that can help."

"Well, if you could give me a moment to explain where we're up to, perhaps that will help give you some idea."

"OK, please, go on. I don't have much time."

Dunn paused, looked down at the table then fastened a stare directly at Da Silva.

"Angelo, people are robbing the game. They are robbing the game of its integrity and turning it into the equivalent of a bookmaker's sideshow. It's my job to find out who is involved and weed them out one by one. Just so we're clear, I'll keep going until every last person involved is eradicated."

"That is great but what does it have to do with me?" The braggadocio in the sentence was not matched by the tone.

"Two questions, Angelo. Let's do them one by one. First, tell me why your name comes up when people talk about unusual events on cricket fields."

"I'm not sure. I'm an aggressive player. Sometimes, it comes off and I'm a hero and other times I look like a fool – it's just the way I play." His shrug, intended to portray indifference, did anything but.

"OK, Angelo. I'll just jot that down if I may." The pause was deliberate and elevated the tension between them.

"OK, question two. Tell me, how well do you know Faisal Shaikh?"

Da Silva's bravado dipped noticeably. "Faisal Shaikh?"

"Yes, Angelo, Faisal Shaikh. Don't repeat his name back to me as if I've asked you how well you know Justin Timberlake. How well do you know him?"

"Not so well. I've played against him a few times I guess."

"Yes, you have. In every game you play against him, something unusual happens. Last time, you hit it straight to him at short cover and took off for a run – your partner didn't even leave his crease."

"Mr Dunn, just bad judgment on the day. We've all misjudged a run in our careers."

"Yes, could be…but I'm just not buying today, Angelo. Something is going on – frankly, you're too good a player to keep having these episodes. You are on the verge of a brilliant international career – it will finish very quickly if you keep going this way."

Dunn knew he was overplaying his hand but felt he had little to lose. Da Silva's manner screamed discomfort and guilt and this was Dunn's first real chance to make some serious progress.

"Angelo, speak to me. Tell me what they have offered you or if they have threatened your family. I can help get you out of this. You might lose some time but you can start again. Co-operation will be viewed positively. Walk out of here and I'll be your shadow – for the rest of your fucking career."

Da Silva paused and flicked nervously at the cardboard coaster on the table. When he looked up, his face carried a strange mixture of fear and relief.

"OK, Mr Dunn. How can you help me? I'll tell you what I know but I need your protection. From what I can tell, the people behind all this will not take kindly to having their prize 'fixer' being removed."

"No problem, Angelo. I'll get straight on to it. Now, before we finish, was Faisal Shaikh the go-between in all this? Was it him that got you involved?"

"Yes, of course. Faisal is not a nice man – great cricketer but not a nice man. I wish I had never fallen for his chat but the money was incredible and once I was in, he told me it would not be in my or my family's interests for me to stop participating." Angelo Da Silva now bore the face of a man who knew he had lost his soul.

"All right, Angelo. We'll talk further tomorrow. How about I pick you up about 9 tomorrow morning and we'll head into Hove Police station for an interview and a statement. It's OK, we will be able to enter and leave discreetly."

"OK, Mr Dunn. Please pick me up back here. I don't want anyone to see us near my home or at the county ground."

Angelo Da Silva shook Dunn's hand and wandered out of the pub. Dunn was delighted at the evening's outcome and thought a late cleanser was in order before the stroll back to the Hilton. "Bloody good day," he said out loud as he took a seat at the bar.

15 minutes later, pint drained and mind turning toward a whisky at the house bar, he pushed back and headed to the hotel. It was not a walk that went unobserved.

Although his immediate thought was a Brighton seagull, it was the trill of a mobile phone that welcomed Dunn to the following morning. 'A' whisky had become three and although not a big session by his standards, it rendered him slightly slow off the mark as he wrestled with sheets and blankets to find his phone.

"Morning, sir, how are you?"

"I'm fine Dunn and you?"

"Great, sir. Yes, really good. Had a great chat with Angelo Da Silva last night and I think we have got our man. I'm going to arrange some protection for him but in the meantime, I'm collecting him this morning and will get a signed statement outlining all he knows about the participants in the fixing net."

"Good thinking, Dunn. Just one problem."

"What's that, sir? Believe me, he's agreed to speak. He just wants to make sure that he and his family will be looked after."

"Mike, Angelo Da Silva was found dead this morning. It would appear that your chat at The Robin Hood wasn't as secret as you might have wanted."

"Oh, Jesus, that is terrible but why do you say that about our meeting, sir?"

"Because, when they found him, they found his tongue in the right-hand pocket of his tracksuit pants. It would also appear that Mr Da Silva did not die quickly – nasty burns to his eyes, probably from a cigar or something like that and his left ear virtually pulped. I'm not completely across symbology but I suspect a bit of 'See no evil', 'Hear no evil' and 'Speak no evil' might have been the message."

Dunn leant back on the pillows and closed his eyes. He knew what was coming next and he knew he deserved every word of it.

"Dunn, tell me what you did after Da Silva left. What steps did you take to ensure his protection from the moment you finished speaking with him at the pub?" The tone was palpably rhetorical as clearly Dunn had taken no steps to ensure Da Silva's safety.

It was pointless trying to mount a defence. "Sir, I was feeling quite exhilarated by the fact that we'd finally made some headway. I had a pint at The Robin Hood and came back here for a quiet drink and to write up my notes. I had no idea that Da Silva was at risk last night and I was going to contact the Met's witness protection team first thing this morning."

The silence that met his response was agonisingly long.

"Well, Dunn, your fondness for a drink and your failure of process has just cost a man his life and has cost this investigation its primary lead. All the great work you have done to get us here is pretty much worthless. We're no closer to pinning something on Faisal Shaikh than we were before we started."

"I really am very sorry, sir. I'll see you back at the office." Dunn replaced the receiver and walked over to his window overlooking the sea. He had always thought the sight of someone sitting alone, staring out to sea, was one of the saddest imaginable and here he was looking out over the ocean, lost in a swirl of 'what ifs' and 'if only'. Angelo Da Silva was just a kid who had made a couple of bad choices, a 'crime' for which the penalty is not typically being tortured to death.

It was a little after 8 am as Dunn opened the fridge in his room and chipped the cap off an ice-cold Heineken.

10

Now, in the middle of an Indian night, lying on his bed in a King room at the Hyatt Regency in Kolkata. Dunn tried to rid his mind of an experience he had relived too many times. No amount of successful investigations or joyous moments in life could ever free him from the guilt and despair. He had built up a formidable track record but the single blemish was very personal and there was no team to fall back on, no other to blame – the fault was 100 percent his. Dunn had been blinded by his need to close the corruption case – blinded by his need for a participant in the corruption to break ranks – and blind to the speed with which people of power can close down risk. His whistle-blower was a risk and Dunn had been too slow and too light – handed in his protective measures, giving his detractors on-going ammunition to challenge his maverick style and leaving him with the punishing weight of Da Silva's death. To make matters worse, the case collapsed and Faisal Shaikh, the man he knew was knee-deep in the whole matter, slipped the net, ready to continue his cricket career and craft an even more complex network of opportunists.

Years later and despite assiduous surveillance, Shaikh was still lurking in the shadows. Could he be involved with in the death of Mistry? If so, did this mean Mistry was part of the match-fixing web? Many pillow adjustments and several chapters of his book later, Dunn finally returned to a troubled sleep.

11

Trinnick was growing impatient as he buttered his toast (cooked one side) and poured his cup of English breakfast tea. Punctuality was a non-negotiable and 7 meant 7, not 10 after. He was relieved to see Dunn making a hurried path from the buffet and raised his eyebrows by way of greeting.

"Morning, sir. Sleep well?"

"Very well. Thanks, Mike. And you?"

"Marvellous, thanks. Right to the bell. Going hard on the buffet then, sir?"

"I'm happy to eat modestly, Mike. You're getting full value I see."

Dunn eyed his breakfast – a mound of scrambled eggs, a few rashers of bacon, a generous helping of mushrooms and a rogue hash brown all but camouflaged his plate.

"Never know when your next meal might be, sir."

"Indeed."

Dunn had sound table manners but tended to eat as if his food might evaporate, a method which suited Trinnick, who was keen to be at Eden Gardens before Kolkata's roads became completely strangled.

The journey to the crime scene was slightly more merciful than expected and they covered the 14 kilometres in just under an hour. En route, Dunn noticed a sign proclaiming Kolkata as the City of Joy – might want to ask Pradip Mistry about that – but was amazed at the expanse of parks and sporting facilities they drove past enroute to the cricket ground. Although Kolkata had a reputation for pollution in many forms, the sky was clear and the heat was tolerable as they made their way to the administrative centre.

It was a day to continue their questioning of the various witnesses, potential aiders and abettors of the crime and the balance of the Indian cricket team. Dunn was looking forward to catching up with Abhishek Misra, who he would put his house on not being involved and who could definitely make a few things happen to assist the investigation.

Pleasingly, Misra was in the meeting room when they walked in. A tallish man, he looked particularly stylish in light-coloured linen trousers, an eye-dazzling white shirt and a pair of caramel-coloured loafers.

"Mike, how are you? Good to see you again. It's been a while."

"Sure has, Abhi. Not since you were smashing some poor Old Haileyburians around the oval at Cheltenham."

"Ha! I seem to remember you doing pretty well that day too, Mike – a classy knock."

"Always generous, Abhi. Let me introduce you to Guy Trinnick. Guy is leading the investigation and is keen to chat to you specifically but also generally in terms of garnering some local support for what we are doing."

"Pleased to meet you, Guy. Let's make a start. I believe they have set up the boardroom through here." Misra gestured to the door in front of them and led them through to a magnificent room which overlooked the ground and contained a bar that would have been at home in a five-star hotel. A waiter produced a tray of ice waters with freshly squeezed lemon and they settled into the plush leather clad chairs which circled the board room table.

"OK. Tell me what I can help you with."

"Abhi, just talk us through that morning if you would. Try and remember anything that seemed odd, unfamiliar faces, that sort of thing."

"Hmm. It was really just like a normal start to a Test Match – a lot of noise, Harish going mad at the start of the innings and basically the crowd just waiting for Pradip to come out. There are always lots of people about – sponsors, officials, friends of players. I tend just to blank it all out and do my own preparation. A group of us were in here signing bats and things. We have so many requests we just grab half an hour here and there to get things done. I wasn't anticipating batting prior to drinks so thought it might be a good opportunity."

"If you could give us the names of the players who were with you, that would be appreciated," said Trinnick. "We've got pretty good CCTV footage but your recollections would be useful. The more people we can eliminate, the closer we are to apprehending someone, obviously."

"Sure, I'll write them down for you. One thing I did notice when we were on the field before the start of play was Faisal Shaikh, talking to a couple of what I would call 'undesirables' – you know the type, wrap-around-shades and garish clothing. Given his reputation, it looked more than a bit suspicious."

The name 'Faisal Shaikh' stabbed at Dunn. *That bastard,* he thought, *but he knew Shaikh was out in the middle of the oval at the time of the murder. Even so, it might be worth tracking the little slime-ball down and finding out who he was talking to and why.*

"OK, Abhi, the other thing we need a hand on is convincing Bharat Patel that we are on the same team. If you could have a word, it might just give us some more momentum in this investigation."

"Consider it done, gents. Bharat will be fine. He's a proud man but I'm sure I can convince him that you guys can improve the chances of an arrest. I'd be surprised if that wasn't his highest priority."

"Good on you, Abhi. Thanks for your help. Not sure how long we are in town for but if it works, let's have dinner one night."

"I'd really like that, Mike."

"Sorry, last thing, Abhi – and don't be alarmed by this but we don't know if the killer is still in Kolkata or what his motives are. It's likely that this is just about Pradip but can I suggest that when we have the all clear for you and your teammates that you head out of town – maybe have a few days on the beach at Goa or something like that."

"OK, Mike, security is pretty good where we live but it would be nice just to get away from things for a while. I'll give that some thought."

"Nice man – real gentleman," remarked Trinnick after Misra had left. "Kind of individual who could 'do an Imran Khan' once he retires. Well-educated, well-spoken. Just the sort of character to lead his country."

Misra had been educated at Cheltenham Grammar, boarding from the age of 12 and growing up far from his government official father and financial executive mother. Although they were frequent visitors to the Gloucester countryside, Misra became very self-sufficient, learning to roll with the jibes of the young English boys whose early life had not included sharing a dinner table with a boy from Mumbai. Joining in the Christmas term, Abhishek had to endure a bleak English winter and two seasons of perplexing sporting codes before what passed for the sun began to shine and he could bring out his beloved bat, ready for a season of cricket. Early matches on wet wickets, wearing three sweaters just to maintain blood flow had not matched Abhi's vision of cricket on the ovals of England's finest public schools but over the years he began to adapt, eschewing his initial wristiness for stricter adherence to the 'V'. In time, he became harder to get out than a five-grid Sudoku and by sixth form, Abhi was being spoken about as a candidate for England Schools – his scholarly achievements were of similar merit and a strong performance in the Oxbridge exams would see him as a near certainty for a place at either.

And so it followed with Misra excelling in all forms of university life, earning a Blue, a first degree and a considerable female following. The tentative days at Cheltenham were long gone and Misra seemed to revel in the English way of life. He was expected to seek selection for England but shocked many by returning to Mumbai, wedding a local girl in an arranged marriage and focusing on securing a place in the Indian cricket team.

"Not sure if a future in politics is in his plans but he certainly has the background and presence, as you say. I feel a strong connection to Abhi and I want to make sure he's safe. Well, I want to make sure all of them are safe but given our time together in the past, it is more personal with Abs. Anyway, let's get on with the rest of the list."

Chatting with the players elicited little of use, confirming that most were with Misra or had solid alibis and that most disliked Mistry but not enough to want to drive a shard of glass deep into his throat. The guards were a little more problematic as admission of guilt meant a likely career-ending inquiry and it was clear that stories were being stuck with and ranks were being closed. Dunn knew that one or more of these men were complicit but if they'd committed the crime, you'd imagine they would have scarpered some distance by now. An agreement to look the other way could have simply meant a photo opportunity, a harmless selfie with a player in return for a little extra cash to supplement what was undoubtedly a paltry salary.

While Trinnick worked through access and security processes, Dunn spent time interviewing the guards in the company of Bharat Patel.

"Well, Mr Patel, any thoughts? I have to say I'm getting pretty tired of the yes sir, no sir routine."

"Agreed, Mr Dunn – perhaps it is time to talk to Bhagwat Puttaswamy. He was in charge of rosters, so he will know who was there or thereabouts at the time of the murder."

"Yes, good call. They seem to have a bit of a roving brief but someone must have been designated to the room."

As they waited, Patel told Dunn that Puttaswamy had worked for years to reach this position in the security detail. Dunn knew that were he to survive this enquiry (and retain all the perks that went with the role), he would have to finger someone and do so with considerable rapidity.

Puttaswamy entered the room with a reluctance usually reserved for a dog awaiting its monthly shampoo.

Patel spoke first. "Bhagwat, brief Mr Dunn about security around the stadium but more particularly near the Indian dressing room and specifically about the men who were posted there."

Puttaswamy leant forward with a blend of deference and authority. "I have my teams work in twos at key places around the stadium. The two men that were on dressing room detail at the time of the killing were Sourav Dev and Narendra Roy. Have you spoken to them?"

Dunn reviewed his notes. "Yes, we have – and as with all your other staff, they saw nothing out of the ordinary and the movement around the stadium was typical for day one of a Test Match. Unfortunately, the stories were so identical, they appeared rehearsed and I'm suspicious that they may have been coached. Anything to say on this, Mr Puttaswamy?"

"I strongly resent the implication, Mr Dunn. I'm trying to help here and will not have you question my integrity or that of my men." Puttaswamy slapped his hand on the desk for emphasis but Dunn was quick to return serve.

"Sorry to point this out, Bhagwat, but there were guards appointed to the dressing rooms of both teams for a reason, that being the safety and well-being of the players, so you can resent my implication all you like but there has been a clear failure of security here and it has happened under your command!"

"Yes, yes, Mr Dunn. I understand this," he replied, backpedalling swiftly. "Let's get Roy and Dev back in and ascertain their whereabouts. If they had been where they were stationed, there is no way anyone could have made it into the dressing room." He produced his mobile and barked a series of orders, summoning Dev to the office immediately and Roy ten minutes later.

Dev was a plump man, possessing round features of the type that would more likely induce a hug from a criminal than a call to violence. It was clear that although he had passed the fitness test to gain entry to the guard squad, he had celebrated on an almost permanent basis ever since. At around 5' 5" in the old money, he was a comical parody of the long arm of the law.

"Come in, Mr Dev. Please, sit down." invited Dunn. "Tell me, can you confirm that you were on dressing room duty for the half hour prior to the match up until the time that Srinath raised the alarm?"

"Yes, sir." Dev had chosen to go with the stone-faced, deadpan approach to being interviewed.

Here we go, thought Dunn. *More of the straight bat garbage he'd had for most of the day.*

"OK, I'm glad we've established that. It seems to me, Mr Dev, that the obvious question that your affirmative answer leads to is, how the hell did anyone get into the dressing room if you were standing outside the door?"

"Yes, sir."

"No, Dev. That is not a yes sir, no sir question. I'm asking you how someone could have got in if you were standing outside."

"I can't tell you that, sir."

Dunn sighed incredulously. "And why would that be, Mr Dev?"

"Because my partner at the time asked me to go and get something to eat. I was feeling, what is the expression, 'a tad peckish' so I was all for the suggestion."

Bagwaht Puttaswamy leant forward and rested his palm on his face. He stared at Dev with a mixture of anger and resignation as the implication of his words landed.

"You've been most helpful, Mr Dev. Bhagwat, please go and get Mr Roy. I think we might be making some progress here."

In direct contrast to Dev, Roy strolled in like a prize fighter at a press conference. His ill-concealed smirk suggested bags of confidence but Dunn noticed the beads of sweat and the drop in the tone of his voice from their discussion earlier in the day.

Roy was a big man with a chest to challenge a tailor's wingspan. His powerful build was complemented by a strong jaw and unfeasibly high cheekbones and it was not difficult to see how he would dominate the partnership with Dev.

"Mr Roy, you were on guard detail for the dressing room at the time of the murder, were you not?"

"Yes, sir."

"Yes, sir. What an original response. Feel free to expand at any moment, Mr Roy."

"Yes, sir."

Dunn stood and strolled around the table, positioning himself behind Roy's left shoulder.

"Now, unfortunately for you, your partner at the time has told us that you asked him to leave the post and go and get some snacks. You know this is strictly against protocol, so can you explain your actions in asking this of Dev?"

Roy knew he was out of cards. He would catch up with that little fat bastard later, but for now, it was time to confess.

"I was on duty before the start of play, guarding the dressing room with my partner, Dev. There is always lots of banter and people passing the rooms and all of that. About half an hour before the start of play, a man wearing one of those security lanyards motioned for me to help him – he appeared lost. I walked over to him and it was then he offered me an envelope and asked if he could gain access to the rooms during the first hour of play, provided India were batting. He spoke English, but not with an English accent, and I just figured he had some deal to do with the players. The wallet contained many months' wages and because he did not appear to be a threat, I figured everyone would be happy. It was not difficult to convince Dev to go on a food errand and I just made my way around to the players' tunnel when the man nodded to me. A minute or two later, I resumed my post and all was normal until Srinath went in and discovered Pradip's body."

"Well, thank you, Mr Roy. I will leave Mr Puttaswamy to deal with you from here. By the way, did you get a good look at the man?"

"Not really. He was wearing trousers and a blazer, a big pair of shades…and he had a baseball cap on – one of the sponsor's logos on it I think. Sorry, I can't help more, sir."

Dunn sat back and stretched. It had been a long day but at last 'Opportunity' was taken care of. Part of him felt sorry for Dev and Roy, who were almost certainly history as a result of their actions. It was probably a scenario that had played out dozens of times but never with the consequence of one of the world's best players left to bleed out.

Dunn grabbed his briefcase and made his way quietly around the group of journalists, who were firing questions at Trinnick. As he passed, he motioned toward the exit and headed across the car park to make their way back to the hotel.

The heavy 'chonk' of a door closing on their limousine startled Dunn and he realised he had nodded off while waiting for Trinnick.

"Progress today, sir, but not a lot of insight into who the killer might be."

"Yes, a good day, Mike. I don't think we ever imagined that we'd have a killer sorted this quickly unless we had a guard with a grudge or something like that. Roy's story is plausible enough. Our killer has simply bought access, done the deed and disappeared."

Conversation stalled and they were both content in silence for the drive back to the Hyatt.

"Right, sir. Quick shower and I'll see you down at the bar for a couple of sharpeners."

"Mike, we've got the day's work to summarise and a full report needs to go back to Dubai. If you could email me your notes from the day, I'll include them in my summary. How about we go our separate ways tonight but keep your mobile on though. I'll need you to be available should anything come up."

Dunn hoped he'd managed to conceal his delight as he certainly had other plans for the night.

"OK, I'll get that summary to you straight away. I'll see you in the morning – 7 am down here?"

12

As he entered the lift, Mike Dunn felt a lightness he hadn't felt for some time. With Alpa's phone number in his top right-hand pocket, he anticipated a far more enjoyable night than he would have had poring over the details of the case with Trinnick. 20 minutes to put his summary together and the night was his.

Having showered and thrown on a bit of cologne, Dunn picked up his phone to make the call, concerned that he knew next to nothing about Kolkata, particularly in the 'spot for a drink and a quiet dinner' category. Dialling the number, he was thrilled to hear Alpa's soft tone answer on the second ring.

"Hello, Mike. Nice to hear from you."

"Thanks, Alpa, nice to catch up with you too. Thanks for your company on the flight over – I had a fun time and was wondering if you'd like to meet up tonight? Apologies for the short notice but it's been a bit hard to establish a schedule."

"No problem, Mike. I'm not doing anything tonight so that would be lovely. Do you know your way around Kolkata at all? I imagine not."

"You're right, Alpa." Despite wanting to appear well-travelled and worldly, he knew he had to come clean. "I'm happy to meet wherever suits," he offered. After a conversation punctuated by excessive politeness on both sides, they agreed that Alpa would come to the Hyatt and they would work out a plan in the hotel bar.

Dunn logged on and began to type as quickly as his two fingered style would permit. Four sentences in, he looked up and saw that he had started each sentence in lower case and gone to caps from there. "Aargh!" he exclaimed and started again, resuming typing at a more modest clip. Finally, he concluded his report, sized himself up in the mirror and took the elevator down to the lobby.

He took a seat at the bar and thought through the events surrounding Pradip Mistry's demise. One of the world's greatest cricketers, murdered among thousands of his biggest fans. Sure, he was not everyone's idea of grace and charm, but in a land where cricketers were virtual deities, it seemed inconceivable that a fellow Indian would take his life. His biggest public spat had been with the former Indian coach, Australian Wayne Anstice – a spat which had cost Anstice his job – but Anstice was hardly the sort of guy to leave a shard of mirror in someone's neck. It was early days but Dunn was certain he was looking for someone who was not of Indian descent. *You're within a whisker, pal,* he thought mockingly, as he raised a long overdue Kingfisher Draught to his lips.

It was not long before Alpa arrived. After a brief embrace, he ordered a scotch with ice and a splash of soda for her and another Kingfisher for himself.

"Mike, let's just go down to Afraa. It's a popular place but I'm sure we can grab a table – it will give you a better idea of Indian food than the Guru Tandoori back in London." She chided gently.

"Sounds good, Alpa. And if it's better than the Guru, it will be outstanding," he replied, defending the honour of his local Indian restaurant, while also wondering how the hell that had come up on the few hours they had chatted on the flight. *Tell me I didn't ask her if she liked curry,* he thought, embarrassment sending a flash of heat along his hairline.

After some rueful recollection of their efforts to exhaust the wine supply on the flight over, they asked the barman to organise a cab and headed out for a night, which Dunn was becoming increasingly excited about. Alpa was more beautiful than he remembered and seemed to be enjoying their re-acquaintance. It was obvious from her elegant dress, heels and a mist of Aqua di Gio that she considered Dunn had the potential to be more than just a moment of serendipity.

As they strolled through the lobby, a cry of 'Mike' stopped him dead. The voice was unmistakable and, with one word, Dunn knew his visions of the evening were about to become blurred. Guy Trinnick marched across the lobby and with a nod and an 'excuse me' to Alpa, he led Dunn back into the bar.

"Mike, I've just had a call from Sydney. Mitch Howard is dead. It's being treated as a homicide."

13

As he touched down in Sydney, Mike Dunn had two things on his mind. Were the murders of Pradip Mistry and Mitchell Howard linked? And how the hell would he ever catch up with Alpa Parekh again?

Upon hearing the news of Howard's death, Trinnick and Dunn booked the earliest flight they could get to Sydney, which meant an internal flight to Mumbai, a stopover in Singapore, a short hop to Perth and then a Qantas flight across the big red continent. They were met at Sydney airport and taken straight to the Sydney Cricket Ground, which, as luck would have it, is only a little way from Kingsford-Smith Airport. Knowing he had would be straight into action on arrival, Dunn abstained totally on the various flights but frankly didn't feel much better than he had when landing in Kolkata after a bit of a bender.

The detective in charge in Sydney was Mick Stosur, a burly individual with a jovial manner but sharp blue eyes that seemed to ask more questions than his mouth.

"Gidday fellas, Mick Stosur. Welcome to Australia. Sorry you couldn't make it in better circumstances."

"Thank you, Detective Stosur, we too are deeply remorseful about the circumstances of our arrival," responded Trinnick.

"Call me Mick, will you, fellas? There's no need to overdo the formal stuff. C'mon, I'll take you down to where Mitchy copped it." With that he turned and ambled towards the cricket nets, his rolling gait making him brush against the rose bushes which lined the path.

The body had been taken to the mortuary and the scene of Howard's death had been quickly sealed off. They sauntered down a narrow corridor and into the hangar-like building that housed the indoor nets at the SCG.

"What we know is that Mitch was batting and whoever was feeding the bowling machine has lined him up and basically fired balls at him. Two strikes, one to the throat and what we believe was the killer blow to the temple."

"Interesting mode of dismissal," remarked Dunn, which was greeted with an arctic stare from Trinnick.

Stosur too was immune to Dunn's sense of humour and continued his summary. "Unfortunately, Mitch had been batting for so long, there weren't too many keen to hang around and man the machine. No one knows who was in here with him and because Mitch usually showers and lets himself out, it was no surprise that his car was still outside until quite late."

Dunn took in the scene and made a note of the exit and entry points to the building. Without turning his head, he addressed Trinnick.

"Guy, do you think there's a connection between Mistry and Howard?"

"Not sure, Mike. Tell what you're thinking. Is there a connection for you?"

"It's a bit early to say. All we know is that we've got two of the world's best players under a forensic knife with no apparent motive for either killing. The odd punter might be jealous but they're more likely to stalk them or send death threats rather than do anything about it. It's possible to have been in Kolkata and Sydney to commit these crimes but a serial killer of test cricketers seems a bit of a stretch. Problem is, sir, I don't believe in coincidences."

"Mike." It was Mick Stosur's turn to offer a view. "Everyone knows that Mistry was a prick – he had more enemies than a New South Wales supporter in a Toowoomba pub but Mitchy was a good bastard. Yes, he was tough on people at times but he did a lot of good in the community and kept a pretty low profile away from cricket. I can't see that they are linked in terms of motive. I think we've got to view these as separate events for the moment but if I were a test cricketer, I'd be checking the windows at night."

"But that's just it, Mick. These murders didn't occur in the middle of the night down some dark alley. They weren't the result of a drug deal gone wrong or revenge for a child pornography scandal. These murders have happened at their place of work. They've been clinically executed in a manner which seems personal to me. I just can't get the answer to why?"

Detective Stosur drove the English investigators to their hotel, The Fullerton in Martin Place. After checking in and having their bags taken to their rooms, they made their way down to Circular Quay to take in some sea air and go over what they had so far. Sadly, it wasn't much.

They bought a couple of Crown Lagers at the Opera Bar and leant over the stone wall bordering the promenade. With the Opera House to their right and the Harbour Bridge directly across the water in front of them, it was one of the great venues in the world to enjoy a cold one, provided, of course, you weren't investigating murders.

As was Trinnick's want, Dunn started the summation. "Two test cricketers murdered within 72 hours. No apparent link in terms of motive but in terms of method, we're talking brutal and vindictive. Who can we say for certain was at both places?"

Trinnick finished pouring his lager in to a schooner glass and stared out across the water.

"I've been thinking about that and I've come up with one definite and a couple of possibilities. Malcolm Fitch was the third umpire for the match in Kolkata and he returned home to Sydney immediately after the game was abandoned. The others, which we'll have to do some checking on, are the journos. There were no doubt plenty of them at the Mistry Test. It's just a question of how many would have headed this way to report on the Aussie squad and pre-season preparation. Howard was poised to break Ponting's record sometime during the series so there's bound to be a few of them floating about."

"How do we get hold of Mr Fitch then? Interesting that he was in both places, even if he was almost certainly in the umpire's booth when Mistry was murdered. He's had run-ins with both players and at times, it has got quite nasty. Howard's had a running battle with him since he first played state cricket and Mistry has publicly doubted his competence as an umpire on more than one occasion."

"Yes, maybe so, sir, but Mistry's taunts aren't the sort of material that would drive one to murder unless his place on the panel was being called into question. Umpires can be a funny breed but I haven't met any that are psychopathic. Billy Bowden was a bit quirky and Darrel Hair had some famous run-ins but most are pretty anonymous in the scheme of things."

"Granted, Mike, but he was there and he was in the stand. Who knows what he might have seen? The Indians spoke to him at the time but let's go and have a chat with Mr Fitch. Different questions might bring us closer or at least give us a starting point."

After hitting the pillow like a man on the wrong end of heavyweight punch, Dunn woke refreshed but in need of some thinking time. Jogging up Pitt St, he turned left at Market St and made his way through Hyde Park to the Cook and Phillip centre for a swim. The cool clear water was just what his body craved and a few laps gave him time to assess where they were. It didn't take him long to realise they were buggered. If these were separate murders, then fine, throw them back in the hands of the local jurisdiction and they can work on them as a crime on a citizen. If it was a crime against cricket, things were a lot dicier – still no closer to why and no reason to believe that the killer wouldn't continue his work.

The morning swim had piqued Dunn's appetite and a plate of scrambled eggs was quickly despatched as he waited for Trinnick's arrival. He nursed a latte and browsed the Sydney Morning Herald, dominated by the news of Howard's death.

"Mike." Trinnick's voice arrived from further across the restaurant than would normally be considered civil. "Detective Stosur has arranged a car for us. Let's go and have a chat with Mr Fitch."

As they drove across the Harbour Bridge, Dunn had to admit that Sydney would make a fine place to live. Umpire Fitch was living just off Barrenjoey Road on the northern beaches and they found him at the front of his property in a pair of shorts and a faded blue singlet. He appeared very relaxed about the prospect of talking to the two ICC investigators.

"Good morning, gentlemen," came the greeting from a fit-looking man with a pair of secateurs in his hand. "Just tidying up the geraniums, it won't take me a moment to clean up. I know you were said you were on the way but you never know with the traffic."

Dunn had considered the traffic remarkably good – as a Londoner, it was like being on an empty freeway. As they had made their way down the hill into Mona Vale, he had marvelled at the wide-open spaces and the peninsula which boasted beach after beautiful beach.

Fitch showed them into his lounge and offered them a cup of tea. He was a large man, the sort Dunn imagined had pushed a few weights in his time and his skin had the prunish wrinkle of a man who had spent many summers in the Australian sun. His apartment was modest and utterly bacheloresque, with photos of himself standing in matches across the world being the only nod to art and a couch and assortment of cushions into which Fitch had worn a lengthways body shape.

Trinnick declined the offer of tea for both of them saying, "Mr Fitch, we won't be long. Just a few questions about the tragedy in Kolkata. The murder happened on the first morning of the Test Match. Tell me, where were you in the hour after the start of play?"

"As you know, Mr Trinnick, I have to be in front of the TV monitor the entire time – I was in the third umpire's room, apart from an unscheduled trip to the gents – just part of being in India, that sort of thing."

"So you did leave the umpires room?" Dunn interjected pointedly. "After what over did you leave?"

"It was the tenth over. I heard the roar when Lal went out and was thanking my lucky stars it wasn't a run out. I was in all sorts of strife at that point."

Dunn grimaced at the thought of an image he could do without. "So, you say you were in the gents at the time of Lal's dismissal and we have to assume that Mistry was murdered between the start of play and Lal's dismissal. I don't suppose any poor soul was in there with you?"

"No, there was no one else there. I was gone for two overs, that's all. I'm sure you are aware that a third umpire going AWOL when the players and the television audience are waiting for a decision is career-threatening."

"Plenty of time though to get down to the dressing room and back, wouldn't you say?"

Fitch responded with a pained expression. "It's possible, yes, but that is not what happened. I was straight to the gents and back out when I heard the roar."

"In the lead-up to the game, did you see anyone unfamiliar on the field or around the players?" asked Trinnick, changing tack.

"No, it was just the usual suspects," replied Fitch. "You know, journos, trainers, camera crews and ground staff. I thought I saw a guy that I hadn't seen for years, helping with the ground signs but he was on the other side of the ground and by the time I got over there, they'd finished."

"Well, thanks, Mr Fitch. Just one more thing. You left for Sydney almost straight after the Indian authorities questioned you, which makes you the only person we are certain was in both cities when the murders were committed. Any comment you would like to make?"

"Look, Mr Trinnick, if I'm a suspect, I'll get a lawyer. Yes, I was in both cities but I was not involved in these crimes. I'm a cricket nut, why would I kill two of the greats?"

"Why indeed, Mr Fitch?" remarked Dunn. "By the way, which match are you standing in next?"

"I'm doing the West Indies-Bangladesh test next week – it's in Jamaica."

14

In his first year at secondary school, he was tipped to make the school's first XI, a feat never achieved before. Arriving at the school with a burgeoning reputation, he was given special dispensation to trial and train with the senior boys, a privilege he was determined to make the most of.

The day of the trial delivered beautiful spring weather with warm morning sunshine welcoming the players to the season. The grass in the outfield remained long and the wicket was green and surprisingly firm for September. It suggested a good day for the bowlers was ahead. Placed at number seven in the batting order, he watched impatiently as others staked their claim for a spot in the side. Although, still young, he was imbued with an incredible self-belief, built from several seasons of commanding performances in junior representative teams. He had a feeling that he belonged in the first XI and that he would do its traditions justice. Many great cricketers had passed through the school before him and he wanted not only to tread their path but to remove a few names from the school's record book.

Predictably, given the conditions, wickets fell frequently and the ball was still hard and shiny when the fifth wicket fell. His arrival at the batting crease coincided with the return to the bowling crease of Sean Irvine, the school's fastest bowler and a regular in representative teams. Irvine had heard all about the young man striding to the wicket and although impressed with the record he had established in age group cricket, felt he was taking too bigger step in trying to make the XI in his first year. It was time for a hard lesson with Irvine as tutor.

The first ball was a bouncer of the kind of speed and direction that fast bowlers dream about – pitching on off-stump and angling back at the batsman, at about chin height. The young man considered the hook shot but realised it was on him faster than he thought. In his efforts to evade, his balance deserted him and he ended up in a pile, just in front of short leg.

Despite the chuckles from the slips and a couple of unhelpful suggestions from Irvine, he got himself back together and took guard again. Irvine thought the old bouncer-yorker combo would be just the trick to put the young fella back in the pavilion and bowled a full delivery on middle and off, expecting to see the wickets splayed and a lesson duly provided. The noise that followed was leather on wood but it wasn't from scattered stumps. With a confident stride and a solid push, the ball had whistled off the bat to the cover boundary in an instant. Two more deliveries were sent to the fence that over and when the coach called him in unbeaten an hour later, everyone present including Sean Irvine knew they were in the presence of a star – no one had seen anything like it and this at one of the country's premier cricket nurseries.

Academically, he was competent enough but his life was going to be cricket, so setting aside his cricket bat to brush up on his French vocab was never on the cards. Attendance at school was merely a vehicle that would allow him to continue on his way to the top of the cricketing world.

15

Hearing Mick Stosur's voice on the phone reminded Dunn of one of his early assignments in the police force. He was on duty at the legendary Oasis concert at Knebworth and found himself at the front of the stage, keeping the mosh at bay. The rasping, almost distorted sound of 'Wonderwall' was not dissimilar to an obviously fired-up Sydney detective, who was talking way too loud, way too close to the phone.

"Frank Mellem was in Kolkata and landed in Sydney prior to Mitch Howard's murder," he screamed, causing Dunn to move his phone a foot from his ear.

"Great, Mick. Nice work."

"Sorry mate, missed that."

"I said 'great work', Mick. When did Mellem make it to town?"

"He got on a plane straight after Mistry's death, arriving in Sydney two days before Howard's murder."

"Have you spoken to him yet?"

"No, I'd thought I'd wait for you. He's staying at the Sofitel in Darling Harbour. Shall I arrange to meet him?"

"Yes, do that, Mick. Trinnick and I will walk over. See you there about 9.30?"

"Good as done. Catch you there."

Trinnick and Dunn walked down Market St and then around Darling Harbour to the Sofitel. Walking into the lobby, they noticed Mick Stosur and Frank Mellem chatting over coffee to the left of the bar. Mellem was a familiar face to both Trinnick and Dunn, a freelance writer who loved angles and intrigue and who had shadowed their efforts to clean up cricket over the previous few years. He professed no love for the game in and of itself but felt it offered much to write about. The skill and artistry of the leading players, coupled with their traits and flaws, gave him endless material for feature articles.

Mellem's motivation was difficult to fathom but there was a suggestion he housed some bitterness about his own lack of progress in the game. As a junior representative player, he was touted as a possible international star but injury and the confines of his upbringing soon put paid to that. It seemed to colour his view and players and the game itself were often the subject of cynical and world-weary writings. Mellem had a presence about him that was always on the edge of malice – he carried a demeanour that suggested he would like to do more than damage people with his pen.

"Hello, Mr Dunn," said Mellem in a manner which suggested the tone did not match the respect indicated by the words. "And good morning to you, Mr Trinnick. Nice to see you in this part of the world. Mr Stosur here has informed me that you would like to discuss the demise of those two fine individuals, Pradip Mistry and Mitchell Howard. Fire away, gentlemen."

Trinnick adopted a conciliatory tone, not easy in the face of Mellem's practiced arrogance. "Well, Frank, we are trying to piece together a motive for these crimes but in the absence of such, we're talking to anyone who may have had opportunity. You are one of the few people we can say for certain was in both cities and in close proximity at the time of the murders."

"That is true, Mr Trinnick, I was in both places and it's a bloody eerie feeling, let me tell you. But the fact I was at two cricket venues is hardly uncharacteristic. I was here to do a feature on Howard, given he was likely to get past Ponting at some stage this summer."

"Sounds reasonable," replied Dunn, "but we are interested in anyone you might have seen that was new to the press corps or any scuttlebutt that was going around your group."

"They're not my group, Mr Dunn. They are there to provide readers with a summary of the previous days play – some are great writers, some out and out reporters but I'm a features man – I'm not so worried about their technique. I want to get behind their protective armour, if you will."

"So, this story on Howard. Did you get to speak to him while you were here?"

"No, unfortunately. We were scheduled to meet the day after he was murdered. I hadn't spoken to him for years so it was a bloody miracle just to get an interview. You know what he was like with the press."

"Yes, we do," said Trinnick. "In fact, both Mistry and Howard had both said that you didn't really have a role in cricket reporting and wondered why you were allowed to attend press conferences. Did you take that personally?"

"Not really. Press conferences usually feature captains adding little to alter the conclusions you've already drawn or cheap shots at the media from players whose place in the team has prompted debate. They could have banned me, altogether, for all I care. No, Mr Trinnick, I didn't have great regard for either Howard or Mistry but killing them would have been like Spielberg killing actors – they provide my reason for being. Sorry, but I can't get you any closer to the truth and if you don't mind, I've got to get ready for my flight to the States tonight. With Howard gone, I've decided to profile the West Indian quicks."

16

At the end of his penultimate year of school, he was selected to represent his country at the world youth tournament in South Africa. This was a tournament which produced the future stars of international cricket and performance at this event had national selectors and talent scouts alike taking a careful view of the performances – not just for the results but for the way the centuries were compiled or the bowling spells were put together. Test match selection used to be the primary goal but now T20 cricket had provided players with particular skills, the chance to make a spectacular living without ever making their national team.

His performances had been outstanding through the week and he had been instrumental in leading his team into the knock-out stage. A semi-final had been earned and given it was three days away, he headed out for a beer and an early dinner with a couple of teammates, intending to be back at their hotel for a movie and an early night.

"Mate, you've been in amazing nick. You must be looking forward to the semi."

"Yeah, thanks, but the job's not done. I've got to get big runs and try and get us into the final. We've never made a final at one of these tournaments and I want to be the one that gets us there."

"Sure, but don't put it all on yourself. We've all got roles to play."

"I get that but if I don't do well, the likelihood of us getting enough runs is remote. Sorry to sound arrogant but that how it's panned out so far."

Although the remark stung his teammates, they had to admit that without his efforts – particularly in the match against Australia – they wouldn't be sitting at the Texas Grill in Cape town, they'd be meeting family members and hearing how well they'd done and to keep their heads up, the usual bollocks that losing teams endure.

"By the way, what were you and Mitch Howard going at it about?"

"Nothing, really. He made a few highly original jokes about Kiwis and sheep and since they weren't going to make the semis, I wished him a pleasant flight home – that really set him off!"

The group had agreed to an early one so they declined the offer of dessert, settled the bill and were getting up to leave when a group of England players trooped in, clearly less intent on an early night given the jovial and boisterous manner with which they roiled their way to the bar. As opponents in the semi-final, it seemed they had quite a different perspective on preparation.

"Look at those Poms. They think they've beaten us already." They had nearly made it to the door when a taunting voice checked them.

"Leaving so soon, ladies? Sure you don't fancy a drink?"

"Nah, we're good, mate. Catch you on Saturday."

"Seriously? The game is three days away. Surely a couple of pints won't do you any harm?"

"Thanks, but we'll get on our way. Have a good night."

"Oh, come on, 'Hero'. Don't tell me you can't handle a drink?"

At this, he turned. Two steps and he was outside but there was something about the fat little prick taunting him that just didn't allow him to let it go.

"All right, mate. Mine's a Castle."

A teammate grabbed his arm. "Don't fall for it. C'mon, we're out of here."

"Fuck him. I'll have a pint with him, then we'll cream them on Saturday anyway. See you guys back at the hotel."

He made his way up to the bar where the cherubic-faced guy, who had goaded him handed him a pint.

"Hi, old chap. I'm Timothy and this is Andy. Pleased to meet you at last. Helluva week you've been having."

"Thanks, mate, appreciate the shout. Looks like you guys are giving it a good nudge."

"Well, these things don't come around too often. A couple of pints three days out isn't the end of the world and I'm pretty sure the manager is getting obliterated on Kanonkop Pinotage as we speak."

"Fair enough. You guys have been going all right too. Should be a good one Saturday."

"Thanks, old boy. We're looking forward to it. Don't want to piss in your pocket but if we get rid of you early, I think it's game to us."

"I'm not so sure but thanks for the compliment."

A few slugs of his beer and he was ready to stroll home but as he put his pint glass back on the bar, Andy appeared with another.

"Come on, one for the road. It'll be good to get to know you a bit better. We've got some spots at the county and I reckon you'd love it in England – loads of runs and lots of lady fans. Great way to spend a summer!"

A round of shots appeared accompanied by a cry of "Chivas with a Castle chaser! Get in, boys!" By now, the flattery and the good cheer had infiltrated exactly as the English players had thought it would but their game was not quite complete. A third pint arrived and he watched as Timothy smacked his pint against his and took it down in one, gesturing as to if to indicate that following suit was pretty much mandatory. He raised his glass thinking, *this is definitely it* and gulped it down, slamming it on the bar and turning abruptly on his heels.

"Thanks, boys, see you on Saturday!"

"Righto, old boy, thanks for stopping by. See you then."

They watched as he walked down the small flight of stairs and out of the bar.

"Manage to add anything to that last pint?" asked Timothy.

"I think the scientific term is Flunitrazepam and I think our man is in big trouble. I doubled down on the dose, so he'll be doing pretty well to make it to the hotel – and he'll have sod all chance of remembering what the hell happened to him."

"Well played, Andrew, job done. Now, how about a cognac and a cigar? I think we've earned it."

The walk to the hotel was just a few blocks and he began confidently, buoyed by the good humour of the Poms and their apparently sincere flattery. He nipped into McDonalds as a means of masking the alcohol, wolfing down a cheeseburger and a chocolate thick shake while pondering his best method of making it through the hotel lobby unnoticed. As he got to his feet, he felt strangely light-headed and his first stride betrayed him as he headed out into the night again. *Must have got up too fast, although those Chivas Regals probably didn't help,* he thought, grinning at the drastic change of plan from night's start to night's end. *I must have been dehydrated. I feel absolutely shit faced.* It was the last thing he felt for some time.

17

The West Indian cricket team that toured Australia in 1975–76 was flogged. It's a word fancied by some Australian sports writers as it sets an unambiguous tone. In this case, its appropriateness was beyond question. Looking at the West Indian team and reeling off the names of the players involved, it is hard to imagine how a 5–1 score line could transpire. Greenidge, Richards, Lloyd, Roberts and Holding were all part of the side decimated by the Chappells, Lillee and Thomson. Even newcomers, Cosier and Yallop, feasted on the West Indies attack. The margin was so great and the opposition so disdainful that the defeat did not bring demoralisation – in this special group of cricketers, it brought resolve, even anger as they vowed that they would never again experience such a feeling. A successful tour against a weak England in 1976 – spurred by Tony Grieg's provocation that England would make them 'grovel' – developed belief and from belief came expectation. The West Indian cricket team became one of the most feared sporting units of their time, terrorising batsmen and reducing bowlers to hapless tradesmen. For the best part of two decades, crickets greatest challenge was to take on the mighty West Indians with the term 'blackwash' becoming synonymous with series results in the Caribbean and around the world.

The West Indies enjoyed this pre-eminence until the mid-1990s when the wheels suddenly and spectacularly fell off. Brian Lara remained the remnant of world class and even he had moments when his cricket became a victim of its periphery.

And so it was until the emergence of two young men who could bowl fast. Their passage into the side had not been difficult given the parlous state of West Indian cricket. Bowling at great speed in domestic cricket, they had eviscerated top orders, uprooting stumps and sending the slip cordon further and further back, trying hard to focus on the little red missiles heading their way. In a nation starved of performance and pretty low on hope, the time was right for Montgomery Welwyn and Fullford Chapelton.

After debuting together at Headingly and making short work of a powerful England side, the pair swept the West Indies to their first victory over a major power in well over a decade, taking 50 wickets between them. The English press fell in love with the handsome Jamaicans – 195 centimetres each of gliding muscle, the grace of Holding combined with the menace of Ambrose. Headlines flourished and it wasn't long before their demolition act kept openers up at night at the prospect of taking guard against them. West Indian cricket was back in business.

Chapelton and Welwyn remained great mates through all the adulation and opportunity, choosing to market themselves as a pair or not at all an ideal way of removing the jealousy and misplaced rivalry that can rise from commercial success. They remained essential team men, training hard with their colleagues and encouraging the new and out-of-form alike. Their only concession to their superstardom was a private spa together back at the hotel, where they would soak their muscles after a day's play.

It had been an uncommonly hot day in the field and an uncommonly fine performance from Bangladesh had invoked longer spells of bowling than the pair had imagined when the captain indicated they had won the toss and were in the field. As they slid their bodies into the bubbling water, the frustrations of the day eased and they felt certain they would ease further when their guests for the evening took the plunge. They had met two young women on a recent tour of England and it was fair to say they soon discovered they had much in common.

Norwegian sisters, Sophie and Frida Jaagerson, although curious by nature and broadminded by culture, acquainting themselves with cricket had not featured in their plans during a semester swap with London Business School.

About a month into their time in England, they were invited by a member of their study group to accompany him and a couple of friends to a private party at one of London's popular night spots. The gentleman's name was Amir Ahmed, a Pakistani by birth but educated at Dulwich and familiar with – and appreciative of – all that came with living in a western world. Ahmed arrived at the business school each morning in a chauffeur driven Bentley, dressed as if he was about to give an investor presentation. On this particular day, a handmade black pin-striped suit was matched with a white shirt and a deep violet-coloured tie. Although not buffed by his own hand, his black Oxfords would have passed military inspection.

"Frida, Sophie, you must come to a party with me on Saturday. Coincidentally, it is at a club named Oslo." Ahmed's words settling halfway between invitation and demand. "It is guest list only, so no dealing with the rabble you normally have to contend with."

Sophie took up the affront on behalf of both of them. "What do you mean rabble we have to contend with?"

"Sophie, don't take offence. I'm just saying this will be special. A famous guest list will be in attendance."

"Amir, you make it sound like we spend our evenings at the Finchley Social Club."

"No, no – my apologies. I'm just trying to talk it up. I'll pick you up at eight o'clock, we'll have some dinner at The Ivy and we'll head to the party from there."

"We'll think about it," responded Frida, with supreme indifference. "Come on, Sophie, we've got a project meeting in five minutes. Amir, I'll call you."

"OK but make it soon. I'd love you to come but if you can't make it..." His shrug suggested that replacements would not be difficult to find but inwardly, he knew that finding two women remotely like the Jaagerson sisters would be as likely as a midday snack during Ramadan.

As they sat in their meeting room waiting for their colleagues to appear, Sophie fixed her sister with a stare and an ironic smile. "We'll think about it." Is that how it goes?

"We'll think about it? Are you mad, Frida?"

"I was just...what's the expression?" Putting him back in his box. "There's no way we're turning him down! Of course, we'll go, Oslo will be mad!"

Saturday came and, as promised, a limousine arrived to pick up the sisters and deliver them to The Ivy. Amir didn't blink as 30 grams of caviar followed by the Dover Sole arrived at the table, nor did he seem concerned that they made short work of a bottle of Krug. For Amir, it was all about entering the party surrounded by beauty, a healthy dollop of status by association and then who knows where the night might go?

His entrance went as planned with a barrage of flash bulbs and the briefest pause as the concierge checked them off. Slipping him a hundred pounds earlier in the day ensured he passed through as if he was Harry Kane, not some rich kid who had bought his way onto the list.

The buzz of the party hit them like the unexpected passing of a train. Amir grabbed some flutes from a passing tray and ferried them over to a group near the bar.

"Amir, what's up?" came the warm greeting from a bespectacled and diminutive member of the group.

"Not much, how about you?"

"I'm good. Why don't you introduce me to your friends?" he remarked with a grin that only the most naïve would describe as anything other than predatory.

"Sure, Sophie, Frida, this is Faisal Shaikh. He plays cricket for Pakistan."

Although this was designed to add some gravitas to the introduction, Amir might as well have said he plays Scrabble for Benin.

Well-mannered as ever, the twins greeted Faisal with handshakes and friendly smiles but if Shaikh possessed a shred of awareness, he would have noted that their eyes had passed over his left shoulder, landing directly on a pair of elegant and undoubtedly athletic gentlemen leaning on the bar behind them. Telepathy between twins is often overstated and dubious in truth but neither twin uttered a word as they moved in unison toward Montgomery Welwyn and Fullford Chapelton.

Their time together over the next few weeks assisted their knowledge of cricket slightly and of cricketers greatly as they discreetly followed the tour around the cricket grounds of England's green and pleasant land. The tours end brought an invitation to meet again in Jamaica. The team always stayed at the Pegasus and a word with the concierge would give them access to all areas, in keeping with their relationship to date.

A tentative knock on the door brought smiles to both men.

"You, get it, Mont," said Chapelton.

"Door's open, pal. I'm sure they can suss it."

"Don't they need a key? I thought they were beefing up security since that netball team barged in on us in Adelaide."

Welwyn laughed as he recalled the near-drowning experience among some of Australia's finest.

"No, I left a key with Devon on the concierge desk. They'll be fine. C'mon in, girls, we're in here."

Only one set of footsteps made their way into the room, a surprising and disappointing discovery for the great fast bowlers. They heard the noise of an appliance being plugged in and a switch clicked on. *A bit of music maybe?*

thought Fullford. Their disappointment became confusion when they realised the heavy footsteps were either male or the barman's task of slipping a key to the two Norwegian women waiting at the bar wasn't the straight-forward assignment they thought it was.

A man in a black herringbone suit pulled back the curtain. Solidly built but not bouncer-level muscled, his brown hair was styled in place and his complexion suggested many hours in the sun. Handsome in a sportsman's sense, his face exhibited a chilling blend of hatred and excitement. He regarded the two men with a perverse grin that did not fill his audience with good cheer. From behind his back he produced a hair dryer and pointed it at the two men in the manner of a child imitating a cop in a shootout. His thumb flicked the dryer to 'MAX' and he tossed it skyward, the extension cord resembling an irritated cobra and the dryer itself tracking a neat parabola and then descending rapidly toward the pools surface. Montgomery Welwyn had not listened attentively during science class but he knew enough to know that if the dryer hit the water, not even a rub from the Norwegians would bring him back to life. Fullford Chapelton was a magnificent bowler but that was where his cricketing prowess ended. As a batsman, he was the quintessential number 11, and in the field, he was a captain's nightmare with skied hook shots bringing complete misses of the ball one day and brilliant one-handers the next.

Montgomery saw that Fullford was lurching toward the hairdryer and reflected on his brilliant catch earlier in the day. Ruefully, he realised that seldom had Fullford been brilliant two chances in a row. As the dryer approached the water, Fullford had miraculously got two hands underneath it. Montgomery's respite was brief, for as his colleague looked to secure the appliance, his footing betrayed him.

Sophie and Frida sat in the bar at the Pegasus. A second martini had them feeling a touch unsteady but they both felt that lying in a spa pool wrapped around a fast bowler with a glass of champagne in hand was still well within their capabilities. The barman took a phone call and gestured to the concierge to head over. His conversation was brief and typically ingratiating, in the middle of which he slipped Frida a credit card-sized folder with the panache of a dealer trying to recover some losses for the house. It was a short walk through the bar and past the main reception to the lift for their eagerly awaited and by now regular rendezvous. As they entered the lift, a suited man paused as if undecided whether he had reached the right floor, raised a hand as if about to start a conversation, then hastened out to the lobby without turning around or breaking what appeared to be something of an already broken stride.

"Sophie, come on, what floor is it?"

"It's on the list by the floor numbers – there."

Frida fumbled across the list of numbers, delaying their ascent by accidently hitting a few extra floors. Their excitement built as the lift chimed and the doors opened on to the corridor, where the conference rooms, gymnasium and pool area were housed.

"This way, Frida."

They swiped the card and pushed the door open.

"Hi, boys. How's the water?"

Unusually, they got nothing back but undeterred, they slipped off their heels and arranged their clothes on the bench beside the spa. Sophie brushed Frida's hair back off her face and Frida plucked a piece of cotton from Sophie's shoulder. With a grin and a nod, they pulled the curtain back and exclaimed, "Surprise!"

18

After a couple of days interviewing ground staff, players and anyone else who could be identified as being at the Sydney Cricket Ground at the time of Howard's murder, Dunn was beginning to tire. His support team were working through the same exercise in Kolkata and he waited in vain for an email resembling a breakthrough.

The only link between the cases was the cricketing prowess of the two men and the fact that they were murdered in grisly circumstances. Nonetheless, Dunn was convinced he was looking for one man and was starting to move toward bookmakers as the seat of his trouble. They were the most obvious connection and it seemed inconceivable that both men had been murdered for purely personal reasons. Despite his best efforts and his success in collaring a few, the bookmakers still had huge sums on games, both above and below the table. If ever you wanted to influence the result of a match or change the course of history, taking out the best players provided an irrefutable guarantee. With both Howard and Mistry bearing down on the world record for runs scored, what better way to relieve punters of their money? It was a theory worth pursuing but in the meantime, it was all about the dire routine – interview after interview of Aussie accents and "Nah, mate, can't help you there", "No, mate, I was having a schooner by then, mate. Sorry, mate." And so it went.

With Frank Mellem and umpire Malcolm Fitch the only ones proven to be in both places but without enough evidence to hold either, the suspect well was dry. Dunn was about to talk to the Head Groundsman when his mobile phone chirped – Trinnick had news.

"Mike. I think we are dealing with one person or a very well-organised cadre of professional assassins." Trinnick was notorious for only advancing a theory once every angle had been examined and re-examined and Dunn knew something was up.

"It's feasible, sir, but what's led you to this? It's an early leap for you."

"Yes, but I've got one piece of information you don't have. The killer has struck again. Fullford Chapelton and Montgomery Wellwyn have been electrocuted while soaking in a spa bath at the Jamaica Pegasus."

"Bloody hell, sir. I assume we are headed for Jamaica?"

"Correct, Mike. I've had the staff at the Fullerton pack your gear. We'll pick you up from the ground on the way out to the airport. You've got half an hour."

Dunn switched off his laptop and gathered his notepad and pens. He'd heard Jamaica was a dangerous place.

19

The reaction to his media-described 'antics' was severe. Having been discovered lying dishevelled and bewildered in a shop doorway soon after daybreak, he was ushered quickly back to the team headquarters. It was both a blessing and a disaster for him that the person doing the discovering was the team manager, completing his daily habit of an early morning walk.

Clearly his actions represented several breaches of team protocol, from being out alone to being out late, to being intoxicated to a level that would've drawn admiring glances from Aerosmith. There was no upside to his position and no serious defence he could mount. Although he claimed to have headed out with the intention of a quick meal and a movie later with the boys, CCTV from the bar showed him knocking drinks back with the England team – the shots of whisky being particularly damning. His claim that he hadn't that many and was sure he'd been drugged was given little credence and it took team management little over an hour to make the regrettable but inevitable decision to send him home from the tournament with immediate effect.

He went from an absolute certainty for the World Youth XI and ready to lead his country to glory in the knockout phase of the tournament to the poster boy for miscreant behaviour and taking talent for granted. Duped by a journalist to claiming and therefore admitting he had drugs in his system made things go from bad to worse for the young star. The road to redemption was looking potholed and unsealed as he landed back in his home country. He took his phone off aeroplane mode to a chorus of beeps and noticed there was text from his new 'mates' in the England side. A video from Timothy and Andy showed them waving mockingly, supercilious grins making him want to smash his phone screen. One day, boys, one day…

He finished the end of the home season, settled back to being a day-to-day pupil and returned to some level of normality. During the winter, he was encouraged to take part in rugby. It was the school's pre-eminent sport and his big athletic build seemed tailor made for it, even though he had played hockey in his previous four winters. After some time on the bench, injury gave him his opportunity and his combination of speed and a 'sporting nose' made him a valuable member of the team.

As they approached the final game of the season, vile weather left the training facilities in paddy field condition, so the team ventured to the gym for some fitness work and some ball sports. After the perfunctory stretching and warm up period, they soon settled into some vigorous competition – forwards versus backs, anything goes. The final game of the session was some indoor soccer and he dribbled his way through the sluggish forwards ready to scorch the back netting. As he planted his left foot, an ungainly second rower, unfamiliar with the laws of Association Football, slid in to make the tackle. The crack of the ligaments snapping froze the whole team. His leg looked strangely inverted and everyone knew this was a bad one. As he writhed on the gymnasium floor, shouting invective at his tackler, his first thought was not the week-end's game but the approaching cricket season. He knew that missing a summer's cricket would severely slow his progress and 'slow progress' was nowhere in his game-plan. Had he known the severity of his injury, his screams may have been even louder.

20

Melanie Pepper was feeling rather pleased with herself. Sitting at the Player of the Year Dinner at the Savoy, attired in Dior and sporting a pretty impressive jewellery-to-skin ratio, she was aware that more than the eyes of her partner were feasting upon her. Surrounded by cricket's elite and sipping Montrachet, she could imagine her life as it would unfold. A life of movie premieres, bar openings and a wedding feature in *Hello* were going to be part of a wonderful existence. The biggest decisions in her life were going to be which party invitations to decline and every designer would want her to wear their clothes. On the downside, the path to this life was to remain permanently with Timothy Faxon-Jones, who was in fact the only reason she was at this salubrious function in the first place.

Timothy Faxon-Jones was an oddity in modern cricket. He sported the love-handles and a pot belly that betrayed a life of indolence, punctuated with bursts of activity – as much as bursts of activity happen on the cricket field. Faxon-Jones was as good a wicketkeeper as had 'gloved it' for England, no mean praise in a legacy that included Knott, Taylor and Russell. This talent had ensured a permanent place in the England team as his keeping combined with a resolute but highly unorthodox batting style meant that none of his competitors could either meet or exceed his value to the side. The other 'fat' part of the Faxon-Jones make-up was his wallet. A life of privilege, born of the gentry and enhanced by 'Daddy's' stock market forays meant that for Timothy, wealth was a way of life. As a youngster, this meant new bats every season, as a teenager, tickets to Lords and Wimbledon were a given and, once he was legal, there wasn't a restaurant or night club that couldn't accommodate a last-minute call from Faxon-Jones. In short, qualifications and physical fitness were for the needy, not for a Faxon-Jones.

Six years on from that night at The Savoy, and now, as the gossip mags had predicted, Melanie Faxon-Jones, the Dior princess, was feeling more than a little bitter about how life with the big guy had unfolded. Sure, the first few years were full of the occasions she had imagined, and she had enjoyed the *Hello* coverage of her wedding immensely, despite some unseemly competition from rival magazines that had pursued her relentlessly to secure the rights. Failure to do so meant their interest moved to trying to derail the wedding with salacious stories, with one featuring Melanie and the touring Pakistani cricketers enjoying an uncomfortable amount of credibility in cricketing circles.

It didn't take long, however, for the bar owners and the movie promoters to realise that Faxon-Jones just wasn't on trend. The Faxon-Jones name was far too 'establishment' to sex up the opening of a new Soho bar and corporates shied away from inviting Timothy to their race days and other sporting 'must be seen ats' because of his all-round boorishness and consistently gluttonous approach to the fare on offer. In short, although wealthy, Timothy Faxon-Jones was a classless oaf and Melanie's life became more and more ordinary as more and more people discovered this. Melanie's predicament was made worse by the fact that, at 35, Timothy was not going to wear the three lions of England for a great deal longer. The end of the road was in sight and Melanie needed a way to change lanes.

For the meantime, though, Faxon-Jones was very much part of the England set-up and a Test Match against the touring South Africans was only a fortnight away. Timothy found the drudgery of county cricket completely tiresome and hated how the foreign players seemed to take it so seriously. Despite this, he knew that a few days at Chelmsford against Essex were required to get his magic hands working and ensure he was 'in nick' for the vital series ahead. As he drove up the A10, he became excited, not so much at the prospect of a few days away from Melanie – who had made the expression 'moaning cow' her own in the last couple of years – but that he had time to nip into the Galley Hall for a pint or two with some old school mates before he had to report at Essex. This had become standard practice for Faxon-Jones and although he hated Essex and its unfortunate reputation, he loved the opportunity it provided to stop in the neighbouring county and catch up with those he considered 'of his ilk'.

Nipping up Hailey Lane, Timothy chopped his Jag down a gear and sped through the tight corners that led to the 'Galley'. How he loved this car, the leather, the growl of the engine and the gleam of the paintwork – just its sheer Britishness. It was almost one's duty to drive one and eschew the German marques and Japanese pretenders. No one had the heart to tell Timothy that

Jaguar had long ago fallen into foreign hands – like many of his background, celebrating 'Old England' was a far more comfortable fantasy.

The killer watched as he pulled into the car park at bang-on opening and grabbed a park right by the entrance to the beer garden, which was just a few short steps to the pub's back door. He reflected on his actions over the past few weeks. His victims had to die but he took no pleasure from their deaths. This one was different – he hated everything about Faxon-Jones – the walking epitome of his bitterness, a man who took the fame and adulation for granted, who mocked his thwarted ambition with every hung-over appearance at the crease. It was Faxon-Jones who had masterminded the plot to remove him from the World Youth tournament, so this was a death he would enjoy – there was a purity about this act of vengeance.

As Faxon-Jones made his way across the car park, he heard the crunch of gravel behind him. He quickened his stride as it was usually last man in who paid and more often than not, that was him. As he reached the door, a hand touched his shoulder.

"Timothy Faxon-Jones? Sorry to disturb you. Can I get an autograph for my lad?"

"Of course, not a problem. What's his name? OK, to Michael then. Right, have a good day."

"Thank you, Tim. You're his hero."

God, he thought, *if I'm his hero, I don't like his chances much.* Leaning on the bar and offering what he imagined was charm, he addressed the barmaid. "Abbot Ale, thank you, gorgeous."

"Would that be a pint, sir?"

"A pint would be lovely. While you're pouring, I'm just going to nip to the lav – bit of a long drive."

He meandered through to the gents for relief after an hour and a half behind the wheel. Having just unbuckled his belt, he felt a strong hand grab his neck and thrust him downward into the bowl. The killer had made the most of the flabby folds which ringed his neck and gripped and squeezed with a quiet fury. Faxon-Jones cry for help, became a throaty gurgle as the bowl water rushed into his lungs.

Good God, he thought. *This hasn't happened since Harrow.*

21

Kingston is the capital of Jamaica and home to around a million citizens. Its most famous citizen is undoubtedly 'The Singer' as Marlon James coined Bob Marley and it is a city famous for its harbour, its coffee and its ganja. Although cannabis is not legal, the police tend to let things ride a little, having more on their plate in a city with a reputation for mean streets, even though it 'only' ranks 32nd in the list of cities by murder rate and is positively safe compared with Caracas. Reggae music and Rastafarians have bestowed a reputation on the city which has proven hard to shake.

After touching down at Norman Manley International, on a landing strip that was more strip than land, Dunn and Trinnick jumped in a cab for the half-hour drive to the Jamaica Pegasus. Dunn suspected that the driver may have taken a route which suited his purposes more than theirs but traffic was light and they were soon pulling up outside the hotel.

Dunn and Trinnick had chosen to stay at the hotel at which the murders had taken place and although several floors had been cordoned off, it was not surprising that there were rooms aplenty at the inn. Only the macabre wanted to be around death and, of course, those for whom death was an unfortunate part of their living.

One such character was Eugene Fredericks, who was heading the local investigation for the Jamaican police. Fredericks was an imposing fellow with the appearance of a boxer but more the street-fighting look of Frazier than the elegance of Ali. His head was completely bald and shone brightly in reaction to the lights in the hotel lobby. The shirt sleeves on his police uniform were in constant battle with his impressive biceps and his shoulder muscles seemed to join what passed for his neck just below his ears. All in all, Eugene Fredericks had a 'don't mess with me' countenance and Dunn was very pleased he had chosen the side of good.

"Morning, gentlemen, I'm Eugene Fredericks," he said as he proffered his hand.

"Morning, Mr Fredericks," replied Trinnick. "What can you tell us?"

Fredericks pulled out a well-worn notebook and began to summarise the scribblings and jottings within. "Well, Mr Trinnick, all we know is that the boys came back to the hotel with the team and went up to their rooms. Apparently, having a spa after the day's play was standard practice, so there is nothing unusual or out-of-character about them being in the pool. Some sources have pointed out they often enjoyed company during their spas but there is no evidence of anyone else being there apart from the killer."

"So, there is evidence that there was someone else in the room?" asked Dunn. "Are you sure this is not just a tragic accident?" Given the events of recent weeks, Dunn was sure but he had long ago learnt that evidence rather than hunches should confirm suspicions.

"We have shoe prints and some fibre from what we think is a suit. It's a fine wool of some kind but we are waiting to see what comes back from the lab."

"OK, thanks, Eugene, but presumably anybody could have left those behind."

"Maybe, but the spa and gym had been shut for renovations. Monty and Fullford were the first to use the spa since it was reopened. There hasn't been that much traffic through and the only ones with access to the area have been staff. The other interesting thing is the tread pattern of the footprints. One foot has made a deeper impression in the new carpet than the other. I think the person walks with a limp."

"We're still a long way from a name or even a profile but this really helps Eugene," said Trinnick. "Take us through your thoughts on what happened."

"Well, from what I can tell, it was all too simple for words. It looks like Fullford and Monty were in the pool waiting for their 'guests' and someone has come in, switched on the hairdryer and lobbed it into the pool. With the curtains pulled around the spa, the boys would have had no reason to suspect any danger."

"And who found them, Eugene?" asked Dunn.

"A couple of young Norwegian girls were the first there. I've interviewed them but they were complete wrecks. Although it is still very recent, they have had a bit of time to gather some composure, so it might be worth another chat."

"Yes, not quite what they had in mind for the evening," said Dunn. "Are they still in Jamaica, by any chance?"

"I told them not to leave the island until you guys got here but I don't have any reason to hold them. If they're the killers, I'll hand in my badge and go fishing." Fredericks smiled.

The two women arrived at the police station the following morning. At first glance, Dunn had to agree with Fredericks. Sophie and Frida Jaagersen might have had killer smiles but the notion that they were responsible for the deaths of the West Indian fast bowlers seemed absurd. They were walking clichés of the Scandinavian image – white hair, tanned skin and ice blue eyes – and even had the inflexions in their economically spoken English to complete the picture.

"Sophie, Frida, thanks for agreeing to talk to me," began Dunn. "You are not under arrest or even under suspicion but I would like you to tell me exactly what you saw – and how you came to be there. Don't leave anything out, not matter how insignificant you might think it."

"We met the boys in England during their recent tour there," began Frida. "They were playing a festival game in London, one of those Prince's Trust matches. We met at the party afterwards. We spent some time together in the days that followed and they suggested we come down to Jamaica to visit. It seemed a good idea at the time."

"OK, so you meet in a London night club, hang around with the guys for a while and decide to head off for a holiday in Jamaica."

"That's pretty much it. We are both single, we like travelling and Fullford and Montgomery were so nice. It seemed like a great way to spend our holidays."

"And how did you get to be meeting up in the spa?" Dunn was playing the naive card as hard as he could, hoping to find out who else knew about this secret tryst.

"Well, let's just say we have got to know each other pretty well. We don't really appreciate cricket that much but we were keen to catch up with the boys in the evening. They tried to come to our hotel but were always recognised. They said this was not good in the middle of the game, so we agreed that we would go to their hotel that night."

"Give me some idea of timing, please, and anything you saw in the hotel that seemed unusual. Start from the moment you walked into the hotel to when you found the bodies."

Frida shuddered quietly at the recollection and Dunn immediately regretted the rather matter of fact way he was going about things. These poor girls were just here for a holiday and a good time and here they are wound up in a murder investigation having discovered their boyfriends lying dead in a pool.

"Sophie and I arrived at about 7.15. We ordered a drink at the bar and then about 20 minutes later, the barman took a phone call and gestured to us that we should go up to the spa and gymnasium when we were ready. The concierge handed us a pass and went and served some other customers. We had only just started our second cocktail, so we figured a few minutes wouldn't make any difference. We took about ten minutes to finish our drinks and headed up to see the boys."

"Frida, there was one thing that we both noticed that we thought was weird."

Sophie hadn't spoken until now and her head had remained down. "We saw a guy in a suit – a dark suit – who came out of the lift as we were heading up. Strange to see a guy in a suit out here. It seemed somewhat, what is the word…incongruous, to see someone dressed like that, as if he was here for some serious business."

Dunn was about to suggest that not everyone came here for a shagfest with the home side's opening attack but recalled Eugene Fredericks evidence, including the fibre.

"What else can you tell me about the guy?"

"Quite nice looking. Tanned and quite fit. He stared at us as if he had something to say, then just said excuse me and walked out of the lift. As you know, our evening was already planned."

"OK, thanks, Sophie." Dunn parked that for the moment and wanted to return to Frida's account of events. "Frida, carry on, will you, please?"

"We took the lift to the floor that the spa was on and walked down to see the boys. We were excited and giggling in the hallway but then quietened down and sneaked into the spa room. We took off our clothes and were about to leap in through the curtains as a surprise. But it was us that got the surprise."

"We both screamed, grabbed our clothes and went back to reception. It was horrible."

"You didn't think of trying to resuscitate the victims?" enquired Dunn, a little pointedly.

"Mr Dunn, we could tell straight away they were dead and we didn't want to join them."

Dunn was in accord with Eugene Fredericks. If the Norwegians were the killers, then get your money on Huddersfield to win the Premier League. But the exercise hadn't been a total waste of time by any means.

Trinnick entered the room wanting a debrief of his discussion. "Sir, I think they're just a couple of girls in the wrong place at the wrong time but one of them did come up with something interesting. Sophie, the quieter of the two sisters, recalled a man in a suit in the lobby of the hotel that night. If the fibres that Eugene found are in any way unusual, it might just start us on the path of a profile. I've got Eugene to check CCTV and interview the staff, so we should be able to build something of a picture. We have had nothing to date to give us any clues about the killer, apart from the fact that he isn't especially fond of a few cricketers but now we've gone from a couple of batsmen who had periods of unpopularity to a couple of West Indians who seemed to be everyone's mate. If the fibre from the suit can give us something unique, we can start some elimination at least. Perhaps the killer has made his first mistake."

Dunn headed back to his room with a view to typing up his notes and heading out into the city. He'd been warned to take extra care in the evenings but had a feeling the streets of Jamaica might have something to offer in terms of smoking out whomever was responsible for the death of the fast bowlers.

A chat with the concierge revealed that the KFC around the corner might have some characters that could help and who would certainly provide you with all the dope you might need while in town. Dunn convinced him that information was the only currency he was interested in trading in and decided to wander down the road on to Knutsford Boulevard. Sure enough, a small group of men were gathered outside the KFC and in a condition which suggested a run-on Popcorn Chicken was imminent. Dunn had done his best to look like anything but an investigator with a pair of shorts, thongs and a Tetley Bitter singlet painting him as Joe Average tourist. As he approached, the circle broke and a man leaning on a crutch gestured to him.

"Mon, what can I do for you? Need some ganja?"

"No, I'm looking for a man. Not a local, maybe been seen walking around this area, maybe in a suit."

He showed the men a hastily constructed identikit picture but the glazed eyes gave him nothing.

"You're in the wrong place, mon," one of the groups announced in a way that Dunn immediately took as a cue to move quickly back to the Pegasus.

"You need to go to Jo Jo's Jerk Pit," he continued. "Go to the bar and ask for Stinga. He keeps a track on comings and goings through here – he'll know who you are and why you're here."

"Thanks for that. Where's Jo Jo's?"

"Down that way a bit but take a cab. It's a walk that someone like you doesn't want to take."

Dunn felt that he'd been given the best bit of advice he'd received in a long time and decided that, despite a balmy evening in Kingston, he'd take that on board, hailing a cab and getting a lungful of passive THC for his trouble. He glanced at the scenery as they made their way down Trafalgar Road and acknowledged that a walk would have been a foolish option. A little way down Waterloo Road, he left the cab, thanking the driver for the lift and the offer of drugs, and nipped down the small path to Jo Jo's. Taking a seat at the bar, he ordered a Red Stripe and had a look at the menu, taking the time to work his way around the clientele and trying to pick if Stinga was here or if he would have to make another trip through Kingston.

"I hear you're looking for me."

A voice like Barry White gargling builder's mix vibrated through his body. Dunn did his best to portray some indifference.

"Only if you can tell me something I don't already know."

"Your call, mon – but you don't have long. I'm here because the boys were friends of mine. If you need help finding their killer, then tell me what I can do."

"OK, Stinga, we think the boy's killer looks a bit like this," he said, proffering the identikit picture. "He's white and was spotted wearing a suit in the lobby of the Pegasus – not exactly standard kit in this part of the world."

"Right, mon. I have people all over this town. If he's still on the island, I will find him."

"That's great. We also need to know where he's been. Ask your crew to find out where he stayed, where he ate, if anyone helped him. We think he may have committed murders in Kolkata and Sydney and if it's the same guy, he's bloody resourceful but he can't be operating alone."

Dunn signalled to the barman for another beer and in that time, the seat next to him was vacated, Stinga moving with surprising stealth for a man of considerable girth. Despite no exchange of contact details, Dunn grinned at the fact that a man like that would have no problem finding him if he needed to. Dunn sipped his beer and contemplated a jerk chicken burger. He felt slightly uneasy about going behind Eugene's back but this was not a criminal for whom routine police work would do. Dunn had a nasty feeling that this killer's mission was far from over.

Having scoffed his burger, he hailed a taxi and, on arriving back at the Pegasus, thought that a scotch might be a nice way to round out the night. He was pleased to have made contact with Stinga and looked forward to getting some information that would move him ahead. Despite his enthusiasm for this method, he was a little uneasy about letting Eugene Fredericks know and felt he may have taken something of a liberty on Fredericks' turf. Hopefully, he could catch up with him in the morning and sort things out.

A hand on his shoulder and an "Evening, Mike" convinced Dunn that, in fact, now would be a good time to chat about it as he turned to see Eugene Fredericks on the stool next to him.

"Been mixing with the locals, Mr Dunn?"

"Hi, Eugene. Yes, I have. I was going to give you a call tomorrow but I wanted to keep the momentum going tonight. Sorry if I've cut across your territory."

"Not at all, Mike, I think it was a good call but it would have been nice to know about it before Stinga rang me, just so it appeared we are all working together on this one."

Mike nodded ruefully. "You're right. I can get a bit single-minded with this stuff. I assume Stinga is digging around for us?"

"Yes, he is. Stinga's on the edge of the law in most things but has connections in places we don't want to contemplate going to, so he's as likely to find out something about our killer as anyone else. The most important thing for us is to find out if this guy is still in town. If he's already left, he is probably on the way to kill another cricketer. Now, how about you get me one of those Scotches and we'll call it even."

22

"This is the kind of injury we normally associate with car accidents. I'm afraid we don't have any way of completely mending the damage. The combination of the force you were hit with and the angle at impact has caused irreparable damage. You'll need to do extensive physiotherapy, and even then, it's likely you'll have a limp."

Rehab was slow, repetitive and painful. A process which only added to his fury.

His knee hadn't healed anything like the possibilities outlined by the surgeon, an unorthodox operator named Max LaFarge who had built a reputation fixing knees for NFL players on their last roll of the dice. He was getting more than an inkling that Mr LaFarge may not have been all he purported to be.

It was the following April before he caught up with a few of his former teammates for a barbeque at their First XV team manager's house. All the boys were pleased to see him and were sympathetic and encouraging in equal measure except a guy called Justin Ilesman, who could offer little more than "Bit of a limp, bro" and an impression of a disabled person walking.

He nodded and forced a smile, but inwardly he raged. This fool had no idea – and for the first time, thoughts of revenge began to form.

23

Tristan Gallagher parked his MG outside the Galley and made a quick check in the mirror before climbing out. The public-school boy complexion was still nicely intact and his lavender Prince of Wales check Turnbull and Asser shirt looked sharp with his navy Austin Reed trousers. He flashed himself a quick smile and strolled across the car park in a manner that suggested money. Noting the Faxon-Jones car, he tried to remember the last time, if ever, that the big guy had made it to the pub first. Faxon-Jones was better at keeping wicket than keeping time and it was not uncommon for the boys to be two or three pints down and contemplating an order of Braughing sausage egg and chips, before he would amble in, bemoaning the traffic, the weather or some other encumbrance. No apologies were ever forthcoming – Faxon-Jones didn't really do 'Sorry'.

Noticing an undisturbed pint on the bar, Gallagher assumed that Timothy had ordered, so he too grabbed a pint of Abbot and a couple of packets of pork scratchings. The stools at the bar were at his disposal, so he hopped up and prepared for an enjoyable session with the England 'keeper'. Halfway through his first pint, Gallagher felt that Faxon-Jones had had quite enough time on the throne. He was buggered if he was going to sit alone at the bar like some Nigel-No-Mates. The only redeeming feature of this time alone was the presence of young Alice Bass, who worked at the bar in the university holidays. Sadly, Alice wasn't reciprocating the attraction and Gallagher could see that her attention meter had expired, so he braced himself and headed off to the gents, not only to relieve himself but also to find out where the hell Faxon-Jones had got to. Entering the loo, he could see that indeed the cubicle door was shut and his suspicion that Faxon-Jones was embarking on a quiet session with the Times crossword was vindicated.

"Come on, Fax, I've been drinking on my own for 20 bloody minutes. If it weren't for young Alice behind the bar, I would have hit the road by now."

Tristan expected the usual Faxon-Jones retort to fly back over the cubicle wall. Instead of the usual 'sod off' or 'eight-letter word for white wine, ends in G', nothing.

"Fax? Are you OK? C'mon, old boy, stop playing the fool," implored Gallagher, but still the cubicle remained silent.

Becoming slightly worried, Gallagher bent down to see if he could determine that it was indeed Timothy in the gents. The last thing he wanted to do was barge in on some constipated octogenarian. Sure enough, a pair of size ten Boss brogues revealed themselves, but strangely, they were facing the wrong way as if Timothy was sitting in reverse. "Shit," he cursed and slammed his shoulder into the cubicle door. "Oh, Christ, Fax. What the hell?" he screamed, not knowing that a response would not be forthcoming.

24

It was another glorious Kingston morning and Dunn and Trinnick were in the lobby waiting for Eugene Fredericks to take them to the local police headquarters. "If this guy in the suit has anything to do with it, we've at least got a raw description. Tall, well-built and perhaps with a penchant for fine clothes," said Dunn.

"That's pretty optimistic, Mike," responded Trinnick. "We may have a connection on the suit but wearing inappropriate clothing in a tourist destination would land half the British population in the interview room. We don't even know if there's a link or a lead to be had. Knowing our luck to date, it'll be a Marks and Spencer's, charcoal-grey, size medium – one of several hundred thousand."

Dunn's optimism was momentarily extinguished but as he pondered the apparent hopelessness of the situation, a well-built man in blazer and tie strode into the hotel. Dunn virtually leapt from his chair to reacquaint himself with Mr Malcolm Fitch.

"Malcolm, how are you? You and death seem to be going together these days."

"Hello, Mr Dunn. Bloody tragedy, isn't it? Couple of great blokes and great players too. I'm sure you are well aware of the fact that I was at a function across town when all this happened, so you can put a lid on the 'death and me going together' crap."

Indeed, Fitch's whereabouts was one of the first things Trinnick and Dunn had checked since getting to Jamaica and his evening with a group of fellow officials left him well away from the murder scene.

"Someone can verify both your time of arrival and your departure – including to and from your hotel?" Dunn didn't like Fitch. He was just a bit sure of himself and although professing a profound love for the game, he didn't seem especially moved about the demise of four of its finest players.

"Plenty of people saw me at the function but I don't know if anyone can verify my taxi rides."

"Which doesn't exactly put your alibi in the water-tight category, does it?"

"No, but I did pay for a round of drinks after midnight, Mr Dunn, which, again, I'm sure you've checked."

"Indeed. But before you go, Mr Fitch, can I just get a fibre from that blazer of yours? I'd like to run a final check. What brand is it by the way?"

"You can get a fibre if you take it without knackering the jacket – it's made by Country Road. They're quite big in Australia."

As Dunn tried his best, Saville Row impersonation, Eugene Fredericks burst into the lobby. For the ultra-cool Mr Fredericks to even break into a trot, something big must have happened, and Trinnick and Dunn converged with equal haste.

"What is it, Eugene?"

"We've found something interesting out about that fibre we found but I'll tell you about that later. We've just got news through from London. They've found the English wicketkeeper, Faxon-Jones, face down in a toilet. He's been murdered."

25

Fredericks and Dunn dropped Trinnick at the airport and headed for a coffee at Danny's Marina. They'd agreed that Trinnick should head to London immediately and lead the initial enquiries into Faxon-Jones' death. It was clear the killer was well ahead of them but some time in Kingston might give them a lead on identity or motive – anything that might get change their current *mode d'emploi* of mopping up crime scenes.

It was unusually warm even for Kingston and Dunn felt a bead of sweat roll down his back and nestle where his belt met the top of his buttocks. He always had a propensity to sweat and warm temperatures combined with more than a dram or two of Scotch were two of the stronger candidates for setting the pores in motion. A coffee wasn't the ideal antidote but it was helping with the headache and the bleariness from the nightcaps that had ended the previous evening. Fredericks eyed Dunn with curiosity.

"Mike, you OK? Can I get you a water?"

"No, Eugene, I'm fine, thank you. Just a tad warm and you turning 'a scotch' into 'let's finish the bottle' has left me on the dusty side."

Fredericks grinned widely. "I'd heard you were a man who enjoyed a drink, thought you might back up a bit better than this. C'mon, we've got to meet Stinga downtown."

"That's quick work. This Stinga could be a godsend."

"Let's wait to hear what he has to say but, yes, Stinga has been very helpful in a number of situations."

The ten-minute drive to Downtown was traffic-free and hugged the sea all the way. Dunn sat with the window down, trying to get a breeze through his mind and thinking about returning in better circumstances. They got a park on Orange Street and sat down, waiting for Stinga to make his appearance.

It was only moments before Stinga strolled in, earpiece in place and having one of dozens of conversations a man like Stinga would have every day. He wore a Chicago Bulls singlet, black shorts and an eclectic selection of jewellery. A Steeler's cap worn backward and a pair of Oakley Crossrange XLs completed the look.

A handshake that resembled a dance move was completed with Fredericks.

"Eugene, what's up?" Stinga's deep baritone surged through the café.

He turned to Dunn with a grin that suggested he knew on sight that Dunn was battling a hangover that would have sent lesser men to bed for a week.

"Englishman, how are you?"

"We're good Stinga," replied Fredericks. "What's news?"

"Good and bad for you guys. Bad news is that he is gone, baby, gone. Looks like he got a charter to Miami and from there, well, that's where my network ends, so who knows."

Dunn leaned across the table. "OK, does that mean we have the name of the company, a pilot or air-crew that we can talk to?"

"That it does but I wouldn't count on anything concrete. It's amazing how forgetful these people can be when the money is right."

"That's good, Stinga. We'll go and talk to them anyway. So, what was the good news?"

"A couple of my boys saw him or at least it sounds close to the person Eugene described to me. Tall, tanned, looked like he could take care of himself but they said he walked like he had some kind of injury. Better still, a waiter at The Four Seasons reckoned he served him dinner the night before the murders. Said he spoke English but with an accent he hadn't heard before."

"OK, Stinga, that's good. We're starting to piece a few things together about this guy. He's still a mile ahead of us but at least we've got a feeling for what he looks like. I'm going to head over to the Four Seasons and see if we can get any more on him. I've got to say, he's got an air of Frank Mellem about him."

Dunn reached into his pocket and unfolded some US dollars, which he handed to Stinga in a manner which he hoped was vaguely 'street'. Fredericks reached for his pocket at the same time but Dunn raised a palm. "On me, Eugene. Thanks for your help Stinga."

"All good, Mr Dunn. Good luck with the search."

Eugene got to his feet and nodded toward the door. "OK, Mike. I'll drop you at the hotel then I'll head to the airport and see if we can extract something from these charter guys. I'll get back to meet you in an hour or so and after that, I think it's time to head home, my friend. Not much doubt that your man is now in England."

Later that morning, Dunn entered the Four Seasons looking for a waiter with the unlikely moniker of 'Lo-down' which he imagined meant he was the source of all manner of information.

He took a seat at one of the sofas in the lobby and was contemplating an iced water and a BLT for lunch when a muscular but extremely diminutive man appeared beside him.

"Lo-down?" ventured Dunn, hoping the nick name had been minted in jest.

"That me," he replied, taking a seat beside Dunn.

"Stinga tells me you came across an interesting guest earlier in the week. Can you describe him to me?"

"Just a normal white man until it came time to walk and talk. He walked like a ruined man even though his face was only about your age."

"And what about his accent? Stinga said he spoke English."

"That he did but not like an Englishman or even like some of the Aussies that come through here. Kind of rough on the vowels, if you know what I mean."

Dunn recalled playing cricket with a couple of New Zealanders in his youth, one from the South Island in particular that made 'kind of rough on the vowels' an understatement.

"OK, Lo-down," he said as he jotted a couple of details down. "What else can you tell me?"

"Not much really – the man had some cheddar, for sure, but other than that, just another businessman."

"Cheddar?"

"Money, mon. Like, no problem to drop hundreds on wine with dinner."

"Did he ask you anything about the city or where he could buy certain things?"

"Not that I recall, although he did ask where the cricketers usually stayed when they were in town."

26

Despite Trinnick beating Dunn to the departure gate from Jamaica, the vicissitudes of connecting flights and delays meant they touched down in London at about the same time. Trinnick had chosen to connect through New York while Dunn had grabbed the last business-class seat on a direct flight out of Miami and despite the remnants of a hangover reminding him of the previous evening's Dalwhinnie disaster, he thought it would be a wasted opportunity not to enjoy the best of Virgin Atlantic's legendary upper-class service.

Sleep proved elusive once again and although a cognac or two brought on some weariness, he was acutely aware that he was now on home turf. Rather than being a low-profile investigator in a foreign land, the full force of Fleet Street would be watching his every move, demanding progress and desperately needing an arrest. Great cricketers from around the world being killed was one thing but this was about 'one of us', an Englishman, and while not a cricketer fitting the heroic mould of a Botham, he had no doubt that 'England wants answers!' would be flung at him.

Dunn's phone chirped as he waited at immigration. Not surprisingly, it was Trinnick.

"Mike, go to booth 34. You'll go straight through. I've got a car, just head for BA Valet and we'll head up to Haileybury. The body has been moved and we'll check in with forensics later but the crime scene is relatively uncontaminated, apart from some public-school twit who found the body and tried to drag him out of the cubicle. Very helpful."

Dunn viewed the small gathering of The Galley Hall's regulars with a mixture of sympathy and remorse. Their favourite watering hole was now closed for the foreseeable future and had been the subject of considerable press. Indeed, many had been interviewed as the media worked their 'big time murder in sleepy village' routine.

He knew that these punters would add little to his investigation but nonetheless was obliged to talk to as many as possible, the 'off-chance' was as good as things got at the moment. He knew that no one else had been in the pub at the time – at least, that was bartender Alice Bass' version of events. The problem was the direct access to the gents from the car park, which meant the killer hadn't had to come into the pub.

Sitting in traffic on the M25, Trinnick and Dunn began piecing together what they had. Eugene Frederick's forensic work had provided a glimmer of hope. The wool fibre was New Zealand merino, of a gauge used exclusively by local brand Working Style. It was not beyond possibility that a tourist had bought a suit but for the sake of developing a picture, they had an athletic looking New Zealander as someone to base their search around. They both knew it was flimsy but it was something and they were a long way forward from the void that had accompanied them thus far.

Trinnick was driving, so Dunn began making a list of the cricketers who had met their demise.

"All these cricketers were players of the highest calibre," remarked Dunn.

"Straight out of the top drawer," agreed Trinnick.

"We've got Mistry and Howard, top-class batsmen, the two fastest and most successful bowlers since McGrath and Walsh, and now a chubby but undoubtedly classy keeper."

As they meandered along in the junction to junction on the M25, Dunn looked at his list again.

"I'm going to get a team together, sir. We're missing a connection here and I'd like to get a few more minds involved."

"Pleased to hear that, Mike. You have been known to be something of a lone wolf at times."

The remark stung. Dunn went straight back to his corruption case debacle with Angelo Da Silva – another reminder that his maverick approach and lack of process had cost a young person his life.

"Noted, sir."

"Mike, that wasn't a rebuke. You've just got to trust that your colleagues can bring perspectives that you don't have. None of us knows more than all of us."

"Absolutely, I appreciate that, sir. I thought I'd bring in Lucinda Wright and Gordon Landolfi, brief them on what we know to date and see if they can help us get ahead of this guy."

"That sounds like a good team, Mike, you and Gordon have had some great wins together. Assuming you and Lucinda are getting on well these days?"

"Fine, thanks, sir. Looking forward to working with her again. I'll soon find out if the feeling is mutual."

The rest of the drive was conducted in relative silence, although Dunn had the distinct feeling that Trinnick had something else on his mind. As they pulled up outside his house, Trinnick uncharacteristically killed the engine.

"Mike, this case is hugely important personally. If we get a conviction, my promotion is virtually rubber stamped. You know this is pretty much my life, so whatever you can do, you know I will be eternally grateful."

"Of course, sir. You know we are after this with everything we've got. Thanks for the ride."

Dunn wandered over the old stone pavers to his building's front door and reached for his security pass. He fumbled through his jacket pockets and realising it wasn't there hit Mrs Trotman's number, a kindly old lady who lived next door and was more than happy to buzz him in, provided he endured a brief dressing down on security and the danger lax security habits brought to an old lady living alone.

Lecture over, he grabbed his spare key from her and began the arduous task of recalling where the hell he'd left his access card.

27

Alpa Parekh had enjoyed meeting the Englishman. Although he may have had a couple of years on her, he had sufficient charm for her to be disappointed that their Kolkatan soiree had concluded so abruptly. In addition, he had an ability to make her laugh, a trait she found particularly alluring. Unfortunately, the speed of their separation meant she hadn't collected his number with only 'No Caller ID' left in her call log. Her inability to reconnect was exacerbated by the fact that he had revealed on the flight that he was a social media Luddite, so any future contact would be down to Mr Dunn.

Reflecting on their conversations in the plane and at the bar, she wondered if she should have mentioned her connection with cricket. With her father and brother making aficionados seem mildly interested she was not unfamiliar with the game and had in fact dated a promising cricketer for several years. Touted as a batting maestro, Eknath Ajeda was fun to be around – at least until the Abhishek Misra's and Pradip Mistry's of the world went sailing past him. Unfortunately for Eknath, hours at the crease on the sub-continent produced a technique that didn't cope well on the bouncy wickets in Sydney or the green seamers of the Yorkshire league. Stints in club cricket brought little success on the field but Eknath soon became a night-club sensation at Sydney's Kings Cross, which quickly led to diminished sleep, diminished performance at the crease and diminished interest from Alpa, as news of his antics made their way back across the Indian Ocean in various forms of sub-text and innuendo. As a double graduate in Finance and Economics and possessing a mind like a silicon chip, she was not about to be Eknath Adeja's home comfort when ambition met reality. In fact, were they to run into each other again, he would likely be more comfortable facing Brett Lee without a box.

Happily single for a year or so, she had kept to herself during her post-grad studies but always enjoyed a night out with a tight group of friends on her return home. One in particular, Pari Gajar, had made it her personal mission to find somebody famous for Alpa, which had led to some hilarious evenings with Bollywood wannabes, or aspiring singers who wouldn't make the podium on karaoke night at a suburban pub.

It was no surprise that a few days after her truncated outing with Dunn that the phone rang at her parents' place. It was even less surprising that not only was it Pari on the line but that she had organised invitations to an exclusive bar, often frequented by the 'rich and famous'.

"Come on, Alps, it'll be fun. The cricket series has been cancelled and a lot of the players are in town. Let's see if we can find you a friend."

"Pari, I'm actually OK on the friend front. Let's go for a drink but I'm not interested in introductions. If we meet someone then fine but I'm just keen to catch up with you. I'm sure an update on your antics over the last few months will be sufficient entertainment."

It was just before 9 pm that Alpa and Pari arrived, ordered a Tanqueray 10 each and sat down on a couple of stools on the short side of the L shaped bar. Pari's update was indeed entertaining with tales of near misses, wandering hands and nuclear-powered hangovers seemingly all just grist to the mill for the pretty and well-connected young woman. They had moved from gins to Negronis and were laughing harder and louder but Alpa could see that Pari was keeping one eye in the conversation and one over her shoulder, scanning the bar for opportunity. It wasn't long before Pari's staring eyes and arched eyebrows gave Alpa the code for 'behind you but don't make it obvious.'

Alpa didn't need to turn to discern that there were men in close proximity as the familiar scent of Issey Miyake engulfed her space and threatened to contaminate her Negroni. A glance in the mirror behind the bar revealed white smiles and gold jewellery. *Ugh,* she thought. *Pari's prediction was right on the money. The cricketers are here.*

She leant forward as Pari smiled over her shoulder. "OK, who is here? Are they our team or the Pakistanis?"

"I'm not the fan I once was, Alps, but I think a few of both. Leave it with me. Prolonged eye contact is one of my special skills. I'll bring them over for a chat."

"No, you won't! Besides, you haven't finished telling me about meeting Sachin – how the hell did you pull that off?"

As the bar filled and the groups pressed closer, Alpa became more aware of the conversation behind her. One man was dominating proceedings, asking a lot of questions.

"What are your match payments? Are you all on contracts? Do the new guys go straight onto contracts or do you have to play a few games first?"

This stream of questions was met with responses, both direct and vague, but the questioner was relentless. After a while, the questions became more pointed. "How do you think a player with a modest test record has homes in London and Melbourne, yet some of our finest players are lucky to keep up the payments on a penthouse in Karachi? What would you say if I told you I could make you rich in a way that you can't imagine, just by making a few things happen on the field that might be considered"– he paused for the right word – "unusual?"

Alpa was now some distance from Pari's Sachin story and utterly entranced with the conversation behind her. The group had dispersed as it was clear that some of the players were having nothing to do with the gentlemen leading the conversation. The angle of the bar mirror didn't quite give her the perspective she needed but it appeared to be a diminutive individual who by now was gesturing and smiling at the two remaining players in the manner of a market stall holder convincing a pair of tourists that the replica Buddhas were indeed hand-carved from genuine ebony.

Pari leant forward. "You still with me, Alps? I'm getting a 'here but not here' vibe and you're nodding at the wrong time. Do you want to go somewhere else?"

Alpa quietly raised a hand from her lap. "There's something dodgy going on behind me. One of those guys is trying to corrupt the other two but I can't turn around to see him. The guy I told you about on the plane, Mike Dunn, is involved in all this. I'd love to let him know what I've heard but 'heard a bloke in a bar talking about cricket' is probably not going to excite him a great deal. I need to get the guy's name."

"Leave it with me, Alps. The other guys have shifted over to the other side of the bar. I'll go to the ladies and ask them for a few names on the way back."

Alpa nursed her Negroni disinterestedly, desperate not to attract any company. Pari's stroll to the bathroom had not helped their anonymity as most male patrons eyed both her and where she had come from with considerable fervour.

Alpa watched as Pari flashed a smile at the other group and gestured toward the conversation behind Alpa. After some nods and an obligatory selfie, Pari excused herself and headed back, offering half a smile to the men behind Alpa.

"OK, I think I know the guy you're trying to name," said Pari, her sentence skewed by tension and gin. "He plays for Pakistan and his name..."

At that very moment, their conversation was invaded. The group next door had rolled around the bar and had now cornered the pair.

"Good evening, ladies, lovely to meet you both. Let me introduce you to Gurdeep and Vinod and my name is Faisal."

28

With cricket or any other sport for that matter, now firmly out of the question. He knew that a different future lay ahead of him. Cricket was supposed to have given him a stage for his talent and provide wealth. Important as these two facts were, he'd had another, deeper driving force for success. His brothers enjoyed considerable success in their chosen fields – success which he had observed with admiration but with an unstated belief that his cricket career was always going to top them. He needed to know that when the family gathered, it was he, the youngest, who was the star. It was his stories that carried the occasion and his presence that his mother and father craved most. There were no grounds for this view, no parental bias and not even much more than fraternal banter about who was best, top or first – but it was a view which glowed quietly within him.

The accident, as it seemed to be continually referred to, had clearly changed all this. In his mind the new metric was pure and simple – money. His brothers' careers in merchant banking and stockbroking had realised enviable wealth at a young age and although they had a few years start on him, he was determined to bridge that gap and do it quickly. He would accept no favours and refuse any old school-tie introductions – he would get there himself and by any means possible. While the metric might have been pure and simple, he had no qualms about being neither in the quest for money.

It was an unusually warm August morning as he waited in the reception at Marshall & Co., one of Auckland's premier brokerages. He had donned his best interview kit, a navy single-breasted suit, pale-blue shirt and navy silk tie with pin-prick dots.

Marshall & Co.'s offices looked out over Victoria Park, then over the many yachts at Westhaven and across the water to the Harbour Bridge. The reception area featured polished marble floors, designer couches and a receptionist who he suspected may have been hired for talents other than valuing derivatives in the commodities market.

He approached the desk and leant forward casually as he began to fill out the security register. "Hi, I've come to see Chris Wheeler."

"Sure thing, handsome. Take a seat and I'll let him know you are here – what time was your appointment?"

"Ten o'clock. I'm a touch early."

"OK, won't be a minute."

She pressed the side of her earpiece and spoke with an accent borrowed directly from Remuera's northern slopes. "Mr Wheeler, your ten o'clock appointment is here." She paused, appearing to be listening intently. "Certainly, Mr Wheeler, I'll let him know."

"He won't be long," she said, her accent reverting quickly back to her roots. Her smile suggested he was a more welcome sight than most who frequented the reception area.

He sat on the couch and thumbed through a recent edition of *The Economist*, feeling like he used to when waiting to bat – palms a little sweaty and anxious just to get on with it. As he surreptitiously tried to wipe his palms on the couch, the door opened and a tall man with an egregious head of hair and a chin that vanished just as his face was about to be fully formed strolled into the lobby. Dressed in an ill-fitting but obviously expensive suit, he had grappled with and failed to overcome the dilemma of the portly – belt over the top 'Hello, Harry High Pants' or belt beneath, which exaggerated the sphere. He shuffled over to the couches.

"Good morning, I'm Chris Wheeler. Found us OK then?"

"Yes, easy, thanks," he replied, standing up and taking Wheeler's offered hand.

"Great, well, come through here. I presume Letitia has offered you a drink?"

"Yes, she did, thanks, but I'm fine."

They entered a small meeting room – round table, nondescript artwork and a view looking south over the motorway.

"OK, well, let me tell you a bit about the role and then we can discuss your background and see if we are a match."

"Sounds great, thanks."

"Right, well, as you know, we are share brokers and our job is to get as many transactions as we can. Whether the market is going up or down, we need to convince people that it is the right time to buy or sell and we collect commissions on that business. Now, and I must emphasise this – it is nothing like Gordon

Gecko from those Wall Street movies – at least not for you. There'll be no coded phrases about liking Bluestar, just a whole lot of dialling up and getting clients. We need new clients and we need them to transact – let the analysts worry about recommendations and where the market is going."

"OK, I understand. I get on the phone and convince people to deal with Marshall & Co. What's the catch?"

"No catch, but because you are cold calling, you'll be told to fuck off in more varieties than Heinz have sauces – and your biggest competitors will be the ones sitting around the same bank of phones. Everyone wants to land new clients and everyone wants to land someone big. Anyway, that's the guts of the role. What can you tell me about yourself?"

"Well, I'll finish my degree this year so don't have much of a track record in anything, although I was pretty handy at cricket and have represented my country at age group level. I'd like to think that demonstrates a determination to succeed and a fair amount of perseverance."

"Yes, Mr Marshall is aware of your story. He likes the way you approached the game – says he sensed a certain single mindedness about you. He'd be delighted if you wanted to join but I must warn you, the first two years give you about as much job satisfaction as painting the Harbour Bridge."

"I've got a vision for where I'll be in a few years and it doesn't involve sitting around with a bunch of mummy's boy Kings puddings hitting redial for ten hours a day – no offence if you went to Kings. If you reckon, you need two years, then I'll get there in 18 months with a client base that will make the rest of the grunts drool."

Wheeler was a little nonplussed at the invective with which the young man spat his sentences but he liked his cannon fodder as gung-ho as possible. They either hit their numbers or they were 'iced'– there was really no downside.

"All right, young man, I just need to do a couple of aptitude tests with you. Wait here a minute and I'll go and get the paperwork. Nothing too strenuous, just some verbal and numerical reasoning stuff – need to know you're not a complete dummy." He guffawed nervously as if to convince his audience that it was just a gag. The humour didn't land.

This was not good news. He was within a signature of getting the job but this could spoil everything. He'd burgled his way through his year-end exams but some of his subjects weren't exactly hotbeds of critical reasoning.

As Wheeler left, he darted back to the reception area.

"Letitia, I need your help – right now."

"Sure, honey, you saved me before. I always forget the 'offer them a drink' bit. How can I help?"

"I'm about to sit a couple of tests and I need the answers. Can you get Mr Wheeler away from the interview room, just for a couple of minutes?"

"Not a problem. I'll be through in a minute," she replied, flashing a smile that implied she had lured better catches than Wheeler in her day.

Wheeler returned to the interview room and gave him the forms and the HB pencil, leaving the rest of the pack on a side table. It was time for Letitia to do her thing.

"Mr Wheeler, can you help me? I need someone strong to help me shift a desk."

As ruses went, it was as plausible as a Nigerian money order but sense gave way to ego and Wheeler was out of the blocks like an Olympic sprinter, following Letitia's sashaying behind through the lobby and into the wing on the northern side of the building.

Wheeler's urgency to leave left him with an iPhone to assist and he completed the questionnaires in no time, taking care to miss the odd question but likely to give him a pretty impressive score across both disciplines. He put down the pencil, left his two papers neatly on the desk and snuck out to the reception area, just as Letitia and a slightly flushed Wheeler entered from the other side.

"All done, Mr Wheeler. I look forward to hearing from you. Bye, Letitia – hope to see you again."

"All right," replied Wheeler. "I'll call you by Friday and let you know."

29

Dunn unpacked back at his home in Beaufort Gardens. Having taken a week's worth of clothes for an investigation in Kolkata, his travelling wardrobe had taken a hammering as he'd moved across a dozen time zones following a trail of murdered cricketers. Shirts which began the tour as proud examples of the maker's craft had been disfigured by all manner of local laundries and now looked as tired and slightly off-colour as their owner.

The papers announcing the death of Pradip Mistry were still on his kitchen table and as he opened the fridge door, he was quickly apprised that milk and other perishables of the same vintage had been left behind. After a quick tidy up – best before, good, use by, gone – he jumped on the phone to Lucinda Wright.

"Lu, can I get you to call Gordon Landolfi and get him into the office for three this afternoon?"

"Sure, Mike. I'm assuming it's about the cricketers. Need some errands run?"

Dunn didn't realise she viewed him as quite such a prick, although he did concede that, perhaps, he could have dealt with his appointment over Lucinda a little more delicately. She had worked in her current role for some time and was the obvious internal candidate to fill the role that Mike became an external appointment for. Mike knew none of this and had made some, on reflection, ill-considered observations on the performance of the organisation.

"Actually, I'd like to hear yours and Gordon's views on events to date – you two are both excellent investigators and I'm sure you can provide an angle that Trinnick and I have yet to find."

"Good, God, I think I detect a trace of humility."

"Jeepers, Lu. Yes, I'm asking for help – we are really struggling with this – and there's nothing to suggest that the killer is going to stop."

"OK, Mike, sorry – just keeping you honest. I'll get hold of Gordon and we'll see you in here. You've covered some miles – a bit tired?"

"Not too bad actually. And, really, just have to press on. We've got to find a way to beat this bastard." Dunn was actually pretty knackered but was from the old school where concessions of tiredness or soreness were never aired.

"Can we have a look at the file before you get in?"

"Sure, it's in the F drive. Go to Test Match Cricket, Homicide and then the various deaths are filed by name. See you in a couple of hours."

"Sure, Mike, see you then."

Dunn grabbed his bag and headed down to Knightsbridge where he jumped on the tube to Piccadilly Circus and then made the short walk to the offices in Jermyn St, a convenient location on several fronts, not the least of which being that Dunn could satisfy most of his clothing requirements from any number of the tailors and shirtmakers who made their home there. He also enjoyed a pint at The Red Lion and lunch at Rowleys was always a treat with several lunches blurring fabulously into dinner.

He greeted the ever-cheerful Priscilla at reception and made his way down to his office, where he logged on, cleared some mail and jotted down a few notes for his meeting with Wright and Landolfi.

He shuffled some files and sat down to ponder not only his next move but that of the killer. Unfortunately, opportunity was rife. Cricket tests were played year-round and seldom were there not two matches played at the same time. Could you put a ban on test cricket on some investigator's hunch? I'm sure the players would have an interesting view on that. Could we be sure the murders were committed by the same person? What the hell was the motive – gambling and corruption kept coming up but what linked the group of highly impressive talent being despatched in macabre and vindictive fashion?

The 'fit-looking New Zealander' was a starting point and Fredericks was convinced that whoever entered that spa in Jamaica had quite a limp, so there was one other physical characteristic to focus on. It seemed for the moment though that prevention might be a better tactic, so Dunn whipped out his notebook in order to work through some possibilities. As he did so, a British Airways boarding pass fell onto his lap. Momentarily, his frustration at his professional impasse subsided as Alpa Parekh's mobile phone number revealed itself to him. Convinced that it had been lost in the laundry at the Westin in Sydney, Dunn had accepted that Alpa was consigned to the ranks of the 'what might have beens'. *There is every chance she's back in England,* thought Dunn as his mind juggled priority and pleasure. "Put your phone down and get on with it," he said out loud but knew he would make the call as soon as he had made some progress on a case that was proving harder to make sense of than a grown man on a skateboard.

Dunn was glancing out the window, throwing some scenarios around his head when a large arm wrapped around his throat and drew him close.

"What's up, Dunny? Good to see you again, my friend."

Gordon Landolfi was never one for the handshake and 'How are you' preferring assorted applications of a bear hug, combined with a grin and a salutation which reflected popular culture rather than his Anglo-Italian upbringing. A big man, he always dressed as if about to get in pursuit of a crook and had a penchant for black. It appeared that he always went one size down, all the better to exhibit the muscles which spread across his body with sculptured precision. Landolfi was one of those guys Dunn wanted on every investigation – intelligent, detailed but also boisterous and fun. A man who definitely knew how to celebrate a win.

Landolfi had trod an unorthodox path to his current position, his early career being in VIP security before the whims of the precious became tiresome. He then joined the constabulary, using his experience to develop security detail for members of Parliament and visiting dignitaries. He first crossed paths with Mike Dunn during a police investigation into an MP that had got himself in trouble after one of his extra-curricular accomplices hadn't made it through the night. Dunn had been impressed with Landolfi and brought him on board as soon as the opportunity presented itself. Fortunately, the admiration was mutual.

"Great to be working together again, Mike. I think Lucinda is down in the small meeting room. Let's get into it shall we?"

Mike noticed that indeed it had slipped past three and was annoyed with himself – late for breakfast with Trinnick in Kolkata, late for this meeting – trivial to some but Dunn could hardly impress standards on people if he couldn't meet them himself.

The small meeting room had all the charm of a public hospital waiting room with a table (grey) complementing the walls (grey) and a window which looked out on to a concrete building next door (also grey). It seemed that the whomever was in charge of purchasing had put the comma in the wrong place and between greys Dove and Battleship, there were hectolitres of paint to go through before a change in office décor could be contemplated.

At least in this case he had Lucinda Wright to provide some sepulchral relief as she rose to greet him wearing a turquoise cashmere wrap over a bright white shirt and dark navy jeans. Her shiny red lipstick contrasted with her equally bright white teeth as she gave Dunn a smile that although not quite genuine was certainly closer to the border of good cheer than he had experienced from her for some time. Despite her best efforts to 'be the better person', Wright had struggled to accept Dunn's appointment ahead of her and saw it as a death-knell for her prospects within an organisation she had come to love.

"Hi, Mike. Sorry to interrupt but we'd hit three, so I asked Gordon to get you."

"No problem, just got a bit lost in a hypothesis or two. Appreciate you both coming in at short notice and I'm keen to get your thoughts on this one. If there is a connection – and I'd be flabbergasted if there isn't – I haven't made it yet. Have you had a chance to read the files?"

"Well, we've had a flick through, so we're across the events to a degree," replied Wright. "How do you want to attack this?"

"Perhaps we could look at how and why," replied Dunn. "Is there something in the way the murders are being committed or an overarching motive that could bring this together?"

Lucinda leapt up and began writing on the whiteboard with the vehemence of a lecturer on a favourite theory. "Let's run through this murder by murder and see if anything reveals itself."

Shuffling through the inevitable combination of worn out black-coloured pens and non-whiteboard markers that seemed to live on the front tray, she finally found one that worked. "Right. Let's go. Victim in one column, method in another – then thoughts, characteristics and possible motives in the third."

She wrote each heading in block capitals and Dunn loved the way she could quickly structure an investigation and give her teams a clear path through often incredibly complex events and happenings.

"Let's just get the first two columns down and we can work through the third – there will need to be a lot of speculation and conjecture in terms of motive."

Wright stepped to the side of the board and tapped her pen on the surface.

"So, in order, we have:

Pradip Mistry stabbed in the neck with a shard of mirror;

Mitch Howard hit in the head with a cricket ball;

Fullford Chapelton and Montgomery Welwyn electrocuted;

Timothy Faxon-Jones drowned."

Landolfi was first to speak. "All very personal with two requiring the killer actually make physical contact with the victim and in all cases the killer witnesses the death. No poisoning or other more anonymous methods. Maybe it's significant that the victim has also seen the killer apart from Faxon-Jones."

Wright was quick to counter. "But we're assuming this is the work of one man. Couldn't it be a gang or a group – what about a team of hired assassins?"

"Yes, good point," replied Dunn. "This person, or persons, is getting around the world quickly. If it is one man, he has been in Kolkata, Sydney, Kingston and a few miles north of London in a very short space of time. I know that means hundreds of flights to check but it also means he – or they – have gone through Immigration a few times. We've got some footage to work through unless each murder has been committed by someone from that country – and if that is so, then we really are stuffed."

Wright was next to speak. "If it is a bunch of murders committed by a domestic suspect, then we are better to leave it to local authorities but it just doesn't ring true that there is some kind of Dr Evil mastermind co-ordinating things. Let's go with the lone killer as our first hypothesis and work through that, otherwise we could end up with endless options and nothing to investigate."

"Good point, Lu. OK, let's look to correlate the flights and passes through immigration. The dates provide some brackets for us to work through, so let's work on 48 hours either side of each murder to start with. They have all been committed within a week or so of each other, so we won't be too far away."

"Maybe that's one for you, Gordy," Dunn continued. "Better still, get one of the junior investigators to start on airline websites – or one of the aggregators like Expedia. It will give us a start and I'd rather have you doing some of the thinking."

"Thanks, Mike, appreciate that. Prefer to be doing web searches for holidays with Ange than pinpointing when this guy rocked in and out of town. I think we've got to start looking at motive. If we can narrow that down, we've got a chance of getting ahead of him. If we don't, we're following him with around with body bags in tow."

Wright brought them back to her structure. "OK Gordy, what are your thoughts? Copycat? Corruption? Revenge?"

Dunn leaned back on his chair and put his hands behind his neck. "Hard to go with copycat. There have been plenty of serial killers over the years but this one is highly original in both target and method. It feels personal though. No collateral damage. He only wants to kill the subject and be there at the moment of death. Corruption is always on the cards the way the betting markets work but apart from some records that were going to be broken now remaining intact, it's hard to see exactly where the prize is from a betting sting. Gordy, talk to the guys who monitor the betting markets in the matches the victims were either playing in or were imminent. Just make sure there weren't any spikes or payoffs that would result if players were incapacitated in some way."

"Incapacitated is one way of describing it." Wright observed drily. "Royally rogered might be more apt. Now, before we get off copycat, what about motives borne of righteousness or that sort of thing. These guys were living their rock star life-styles in one way or another and maybe someone wanted to teach them a lesson."

Landolfi grinned. "You mean a bit like 'Se7en' Lu, creepy stuff that! Whaat's in the box?" He delivered in his best Brad Pitt.

Wright grinned back. "Yes, Gordon, something like that. I'm not sure if we've got seven deadly sins here but let's not rule anything out."

"Hang on," interrupted Dunn. "We could easily have something like that. Think about the murders – Mistry, pride. Howard, envy. Faxon-Jones takes care of gluttony and sloth. If some of the stories about the West Indian boys are anything to go by, they probably made lust their own."

"What does that leave?" asked Landolfi.

"Buggered if I know," said Dunn. "Google it."

"Just bringing it up now, Mike. OK, we've got envy, pride…what else is there…ah, here we go. The missing two are greed and wrath."

Dunn recalled watching 'Se7en' with a girl he'd been keen on and acknowledged that it probably wasn't first date material. "If we stay with the movie, wrath was an act of revenge, so let's assume our killer has that covered. Greed and the modern cricketer – not sure that narrows things down much."

"Well, they are all well-paid with their national contracts, endorsements and of course the various T-20 leagues," said Wright. "But perhaps there are some that are more obviously out for material benefit than others. Let's have a think about who we would put in that bracket."

Dunn was quick to the whiteboard. "Faisal Shaikh tops my list. Anything for some extra cash for that guy." He spat with considerable venom. "It's Faisal first, second and third for that little prick."

"Yes, all right, Mike," admonished Wright. "We know the history but, respectfully, let's keep objective on this."

"Sorry, fair call. But we can't rule him out."

"What about Pieter van Zyl, the South African?" Offered Landolfi. "He won't play for his country, just nips around the world putting his hand up for every T20 tournament he can – and he'd endorse AK-47s if the price was right."

"Yes, good – a solid candidate. What about anyone closer to home? Given the most recent murder was Faxon-Jones. There is every chance the killer is still in the country."

Wright grabbed a pen and brandished it at her colleagues. "I'll tell you who is the master of material possession – and moves between women and Ferraris at warp speed. If our theory is close to being on the money, this is not a good time to be Andy Beaumont."

30

"Hello, it's Andy Beaumont speaking."

Dunn cursed as the voicemail greeting continued. "I'm sorry I've missed you but please leave a message and I'll come back to you as soon as I can."

"Bugger," said Dunn. *If I could just have a word to him, I could at least tell him to be careful,* he thought. He looked at the fixture list and could see that Beaumont was due to play for Surrey against Derbyshire at Chesterfield a couple of days hence. After considering his options, he figured a call to Simon Feast, one of his old mates from the Met who lived up that way, would at least provide him with some surveillance without scaring any of the cricketers unnecessarily. Feast agreed to wander down to the team hotel later that evening and Dunn was comfortable that for his time in Derbyshire, Andy Beaumont would be looked at, even he couldn't guarantee he would be looked after. As for the rest of his 'potentials 'list, he wasn't really in a position to warn the authorities in other parts of the world. He had to hope that his hunch was right and that the killer was still in England.

Dunn began to feel a tad peckish so decided to prepare dinner. That meant thumbing through the flyers from the assortment of restaurants in the area and he settled on some Indian from a local restaurant, Shiva. It was a ten-minute stroll and he needed a bit of time to ponder and get a bit of the tension out of his body.

As he threw on a baseball cap and opened his front door, his phone rang. *Let this be Beaumont,* he mentally pleaded. No such luck.

"Sir, It's Jolian Ford-Robertson here. I was speaking to Gordon Landolfi earlier and as you instructed, I've been looking at flights from Kingston to London. Most come via Miami, so things get a bit blurry. I've got a group of New Zealanders going from Kingston to Miami – there has been a Golden Oldies cricket tournament on in the West Indies – but none have connected direct to London. Most headed to Los Angeles and back to New Zealand but a few went to Chicago and New York. Only one person travelled on to London from the group – a carpet magnate who has been here on business. He is legitimate, sir, we've checked him out thoroughly."

"OK, well done, Jolian. Not sure if Gordon mentioned it but you're going to have to start sifting through customs records." He knew there would be thousands of Kiwis coming in and out of London but it was all he had.

"You have the profile. I need a name. Good luck." He hung up a little abruptly, not through any dissatisfaction with Ford-Robertson but frustration of having the killer remain a critical step ahead at every turn. His one bright point was that no one matching the profile he had developed had left the country – at least not since a day after Faxon-Jones was found. As he strolled down to collect his dinner, he couldn't enjoy the gorgeous summer evening. What if the killer had moved on? What if he was ready to strike again?

31

The first six months were, indeed, ugly. Trawling through lists of names, getting agreement to sign up, convincing them of the merits of a start-up that was going to revolutionise something riveting like the detergent industry, then taking their order for $500 worth of shares – this was not the big time and it paid accordingly, meaning his quest for wealth was a slow one. And this was happening at the same time as his brothers transacted at the big end of town, drawing further ahead in his imagined race.

Although not there to make friends, Friday night beers led to conversations with his call-centre peers and one in particular, who went by the unlikely name of Chance Davis. Chance was a diversity hire-wrong background, wrong education and wrong criminal record; all of which made him perfect material for Marshall & Co.'s social equity stance. Chance was all ripple and attitude, his tattoos showing through his white business shirts and his rings (nose, ear and eyebrow) competed with his mystifying array of hairstyles in providing an on-going source of fascination to the executive floor.

Their conversations revolved around sport, women and how they were going to get out of the call centre and on to the trading desk. Increasingly, sport and women took a back seat and most Fridays saw them in the back corner of the Empire Hotel, swapping theories on how to break out. Receptionist Letitia was a frequent companion and although she didn't add any discernible value on the financial front, her apparent invisibility while among the senior traders provided an on-going source of 'oil' both good and bad.

One Friday, as they settled into a round of Jack and Cokes, Letitia piped up after a period of uncharacteristic silence.

"A couple of the guys from the trading team were bangin' on about some big deal that's coming up. Said they were going to bury themselves in some stock, whatever that means."

"Interesting 'L'. Key piece of information here is the name of the stock. What have you got for us?"

"Shit, thought you'd ask that. It was something like Uniplex. They reckon it's going to win a bid to supply the government computer gear but the market thinks Compusystem has got the deal done. Does that sound right?"

Chance spoke next. "L, if you've got that right, this could be a big one. The I.T. contract for the government is worth millions. There'll be big bets on both companies – the winner will go through the roof!"

He held up his hand to temper the excitement. "Yeah but if we're going to get some of that action, we need to find someone to borrow some cash from. A couple of newbies like you and me don't have too many contacts like that."

"Leave that with me. I reckon there's someone who I can convince – someone who would love to see a young fella from the other side of the tracks stick it to these guys."

By Monday, Chance had his backer and it was now over to the rookies to deliver.

"Mate?" Chance inquired. "Why don't you go and check out this info with one of the traders? Hang some bait and see what happens."

"Who do you reckon? Most of these guys wouldn't give a beggar a French fry. I can't see them opening the door for a broken ex-cricketer and a blinged-up Westie."

"I reckon Alecia Cunningham's worth a shot. There's no way she'd suspect a big play from us and I reckon she wouldn't mind throwing a couple of juniors a bone. She got treated like shit when she first got here and she wants to make it easier for people like us, *and* she's the company expert in governmental matters. Apparently she's made some monster calls over the years."

He approached Cunningham's office door with an air of contrived insouciance, which soon dwindled to shuffling inadequacy, as he spied the jewellery, the tailored suit and the tone of voice with which she was speaking to some poor cove on the other end of the phone.

"Don't give me any of that bullshit. I said a table for four inside the house. I made the reservation last week. Just make it happen. I'm sure you're not going to want to tell your boss that Marshall & Co. are taking their business elsewhere." It was touch and go whether the call was over as she muttered,

"Fucking, Antoine's," while replacing the receiver.

"Hope I'm not interrupting," he offered as he leant on the jamb.

114

"No, just sorting lunch. Bloody cretins. What can I do for you?"

"Well, Chance and I were just interested to get your thoughts on where the market's going. We're building up our client bases and it would be great to get something from you to help our recommendations."

"Fuck me, you've got some cheek. My advice is worth a long lunch at Cibo at the very least and you reckon you'll get it without even offering me a trim latte?" A wry smile emerged.

"You and Chance have got some cojones. I'll give you that – and I do appreciate how you managed to steer that lounge lizard Wheeler away from me at the Christmas do. Your names pop up now and again in personnel meetings and it sounds like you are doing OK the pair of you. Look, I'm happy to give you a steer but what do you really want to know?"

"What do you know about the IT industry?" He offered with cherubic innocence.

"Close the door."

She beckoned him in and indicated a seat opposite her desk.

"Breathe a word of this to anyone and I'll have those cojones sautéed and served as entrée. There're some rumblings about government contracts – most would contend that it's pretty much a two-horse race – but let's just say that sometimes the obvious doesn't eventuate. Bear that in mind while you and Chance are trying to connect the dots."

"Thanks, Alecia. Shout you a gin at the Empire on Friday?"

"No need, just make sure you leave some stock for me. I reckon it'll sort out the beach house at Waiheke if it comes in."

Reporting back, Chance couldn't contain his glee. "Mate, this is it. This is our full toss on leg stump when you need six off the last ball to win the World Cup!"

"Chance, love the cricket analogy but I'm not sure we're quite home yet. Two gaps in the plan. Not completely sure which company is going to win and not completely sure how we're going to take a huge position without having everyone in the building crawling all over us."

"Don't worry about the second bit – my contact will take the position. They'll never link it back to us. But I see your point on the play. What exactly did Alecia say about who was going to win the bid?"

"She just said something about us being able to 'connect the dots'. Everyone thinks it's definitely between Uniplex and Compusystems but there's something out there that is going to blow this wide open – and it's something that the market hasn't figured out yet."

32

A long session and some scribbled napkins later, a plan began to take shape. This was not about the technology itself and it was unlikely to be just about the price, as both companies knew the value of the deal, so it was likely the two offers would be similar. Somewhere in this mix was another driver – a human element? Possibly. A political motivation? Probably. Whatever it was, they had to find it before the announcement was leaked and the share prices moved.

It was agreed that surveillance was the way to go. The Minister heading the procurement process needed to be watched, as did the comings and goings at Uniplex and Compusystems. A range of excuses were conjured up and leave was granted so the trio (Letitia would not be denied) sauntered down to Wellington to find their edge. They reckoned they had the week, after which the news would be public and the opportunity gone.

They rented an apartment in Thorndon and, after dropping their luggage, took the short stroll past New Zealand's parliament buildings and settled in at The Old Bailey for a pint or two and some dinner.

Chase was feeling like a man on the precipice of glory and spoke impassionedly but close to unintelligibly through a mouthful of burger.

"Guys, this is the last time we dine at a joint like this." He tried to swallow quickly and tapped the table for added gravitas. "From here on in, it's silver service, baby. Let me show you to your usual table, Mr Davis, I've chilled the Krug."

High fives were exchanged and pints were drained and they went through the plan one more time.

Letitia spent the first two days at Uniplex, managing to report that there was nothing there other than a 'bunch of wankers in suits'. No sign of government officials and the CEO arrived at seven o'clock in the morning and left at around the same hour in the evening. Chance had little more to advance their prospects from lurking at Compusystem but had arranged a coffee with the HR assistant for Thursday morning. The smile with which he delivered the news suggested it was unrelated to the task at hand. His own tagging of the minister revealed little more with trips from his Khandalla home to The Beehive his usual routine. By mid-afternoon Wednesday, things were looking a bit grim until the situation changed as rapidly as it did unexpectedly.

He watched as the minister hopped in his car and was driven north to Days Bay. The driver left him at the Days Bay Pavilion and drove off, ostensibly heading back to Wellington. With his phone at his ear, the minister went inside, ordered a Steinlager Pure and pulled a folder from his briefcase. After an hour, during which he must have checked his watch a dozen times, he looked up and saw the ferry from Wellington approaching, at which he packed up his papers and drained the last of his second beer. A smartly attired woman strolled down the pier and jumped into a Corporate Cab. As it shaped to leave, the minister jumped in beside her. Game on…

It was a short trip to an Airbnb in Mahina Bay and he waited patiently for their 'meeting' to conclude. Inevitably, the government limo arrived and the minister made a furtive exit, heading back to parliament house as if he'd just had an afternoon placating some concerned constituents. Half an hour later, his companion made her way down the pathway to the front of the property and he greeted her with considerable glee.

"Alecia Cunningham, fancy seeing you here."

"Oh, fuck. What are you doing here? I heard you were visiting a sick aunty in Rotorua."

"Just needed some time off. Chance and I felt we were better placed to solve this one if we were closer to the action – and close to the action I was. How about I give you a lift to the Pavilion and you can give me everything you've just learnt, assuming you had time for business?"

"Very funny, you smart little shit. OK, let's talk but if anything comes back to me, I'll break your other fucking leg."

The conversation was brief. Neither Uniplex nor Compusystems would win the contract and Alecia would make yet another remarkable prediction to beat the market. The winner was going to be a relative newcomer who had sourced the technology from the US but would create jobs in New Zealand to manage the contract, a dream scenario for a government south of 40 in the polls.

"Get your money on today, sweetheart," she remarked without a shred of affection. "The announcement has been put back to Monday, so the market will go nuts in the next 48 hours. Get in today and out by Friday – Compusystem and Uniplex will be unsaleable by lunchtime on Monday. Take a stake in the winner and hang onto it for a month or two. Don't get too greedy. The watchdog will spot anything weird this close to a bid. Now fuck off and let me catch my ferry. We won't speak again after this, right? It seems neither of us are where we should be, so let's leave it at that, eh?"

The door at the Days Bay Pavilion hadn't even shut before he was on the phone to Auckland. He then rang Chase and told him to get Letitia and meet him at Shed 5.

"What have you got mate?" asked Chance.

"Let's not do it by phone. Just meet me there and we'll sort out next steps."

It was only 45 minutes later when they flew through the door and sat down to a round of espresso martinis – not his first choice for an afternoon beverage, but the price he had to pay for sending Letitia to the bar.

"I think I've got the steer we need. Don't ask me how but I managed to get the bid winner from staying close to the minister. They are delaying the announcement until Monday but the winner has been decided already."

"So, come on, mate, who is it and why don't we get on it?"

"Alright, alright. Tell your friend to get on straight away."

"Get on who?"

"Uniplex."

33

Melanie Faxon-Jones flicked her hair back as she stepped from the shower. A subtle tan and frequent HIIT sessions ensured she remained a distinctly attractive woman, despite years of parties and associated decadence alongside her cricketing husband. Leaning forward to apply some moisturiser, she became aware that she was not the only one enjoying her reflection. She whirled around and hurled her towel in the direction of the door, hoping to buy herself some time but it was too late. Surging through the door, he grabbed her and pressed her against the shower door. He was large and powerful and as she pushed against him, she could feel his solid pectoral muscles and well-defined shoulders. This was not a battle she could win on physical grounds.

"Stop it, Andy, I'm going to be late!" She protested, as Andy Beaumont's hands grabbed her hips. They kissed, but she broke away.

"Andy, I can't be late. I've got to meet Timothy's parents to discuss funeral arrangements and rolling in late after an afternoon with you is hardly de rigueur for a 'grieving widow'."

Andy was tempted to point out the flaws in her reasoning but realised he wasn't in any stronger position than her on moral grounds. The affair had begun a month before and although he knew deep down that it was 'pretty poor form' to be indulging in an affair with a teammate's wife, Andy Beaumont didn't really give a toss about anything other than pleasing himself.

A product of Eton and Cambridge, life had been pretty good for Andy Beaumont. Blessed with good looks and a trust fund, he had the added advantage of being a world-class batsman. The adulation of women was not hard to come by but Beaumont was particularly attracted to those that, according to societal norms, he couldn't have. When Melanie Faxon-Jones had made some less than wholesome remarks to him at a recent sponsor's do, their union was a matter of when, not if.

"Catching up with the Faxon-Jones – what fun. Fancy a cup of tea before you hit the road?"

"No thanks, darling. I'll get going. I've got to be in Virginia Water by mid-afternoon so I might as well get going. Throw me my towel, will you?"

Beaumont did so and went into his bedroom. He threw on a pair of shorts and a Chelsea replica shirt and meandered across the lounge to his kitchen.

Melanie had contrived her best mourning demeanour and although she went designer label even in death, the charade was a convincing one. Black Armani pants, black chiffon shirt and a Prada jacket completed an ensemble that would drain the average worker's monthly wage but was unlikely to survive the seasonal clear out. Grieving was hard work when you detested the deceased and a broken heart was not easy to conjure, but she did what she had to do.

She looked in the mirror at the top of the stairs and worked on her 'I'm so shattered' expression.

"OK, darling. See you later."

"Sure, see you in a few days. What about dinner at Chumleys on Thursday then back here for dessert?"

"I was hoping to come back here tonight."

"That would be great but I'm supposed to be in Derby tonight. We've got a game coming up there."

"Can't you go up in the morning, darling? I thought a nice evening together with a couple of bottles of Burgundy would be wonderful."

Beaumont paused and Melanie could tell he was warming to her theme.

"Maybe I could ring the coach and tell him I need to skip the team meeting tonight but I'll be there for breakfast in the morning. I'll dream up some personal reason."

"Perfect, darling. I'll see you here about eight o'clock. Don't worry about dinner, I'll pick something up on the way."

She smiled and with a kiss on his forehead, waltzed out into the street and eased herself into her shiny black Porsche.

Beaumont grinned as she drove away. This would be fun while it lasted.

34

The killer prowled carefully down Atalanta St, making several passes before pausing outside Andy Beaumont's house. A black Porsche had sped down Fulham Palace Road just before he made it into the street. If his homework was on the money, it had to be one Melanie Faxon-Jones heading away after a tryst with Beaumont. He hit the button on the security system and waited for a response.

"Mel, is that you? What have you forgotten?"

"Actually, it's not Mel. It's an old cricket opponent of yours. Sorry to drop in unannounced but I'm in London and thought I'd look you up on the off-chance."

"Who did you say you were? Sorry, I missed your name in all that."

"It was a while ago that we played. Way back at the World Youth tournament. In fact, we had a drink together. You guys stitched me up well and truly." He made the last remark with a chuckle, hoping Beaumont would get the impression that no hard feelings existed.

Beaumont felt a moment of unease but pushed the key button anyway. "You've got me buggered but come on up. Just push the door when you hear the click."

The killer ascended the stairs and smiled as he took in Beaumont's clichéd bachelor pad – enormous flat screen, the latest Bose equipment, photos of himself and a drinks trolley for sealing those all-too-frequent late-night conquests.

"You're that bloody Kiwi! Yes, I do remember having a beer or two with you – sorry to hear about your injury. Thought you were going to be quite a player."

"Ah, well, these things happen. How about a beer? And hold the additives this time, eh?"

"Of course, I've got a few that will be chilled nicely by now. Lager OK?"

"Perfect, thanks."

They ripped the tops from a couple of cans of Stella and chatted away. Beaumont leafing through some publications in the coffee table drawer to find the programme from the tournament they had played in.

"Look at some of these names. Some pretty good pedigree at that tournament."

"Sure was, although apart from poor old Mitch Howard, the Aussies were rubbish. Look at India, no wonder they won the bloody thing."

Their reminisces continued at a pace just below their beer consumption and Andy was quick to replenish. As he made his way to the fridge for the third can, he paused.

"Pity you won't be able to catch up with Tim Faxon-Jones. I'm sure you've heard the news."

"Yes, although I did manage to catch up with him at The Galley Hall last week."

"You were…at the Galley? Oh, shit, you're…"

Andy Beaumont didn't get to finish that sentence. The killer had followed him into the kitchen and, with a sharp upward motion with a skewer, added Andy Beaumont to the list of great cricketers the world had seen the last of.

35

He was never completely sure why he betrayed Chance. They had been in it together but when the information arrived, it seemed inconceivable that he would share it and halve the opportunity. A maverick partner had funded his position and his trades netted him millions, providing him with an immediate opportunity to sever ties with Marshall & Co. and start trading for his own purposes. He did feel a pang of regret upon hearing Chance was discovered with Letitia,their respective heads placed on each other's torsos as a clear message to anyone who borrowed and failed to repay or whose advice didn't reap the intended rewards. Although he sensed it at the time, it was clear that Chance hadn't gone to the Henderson branch of the Bank of New Zealand for the money.

As a wealthy young man with a personal brokerage and an office in Parnell overlooking the harbour, it seemed that happiness would be the last thing he needed to pursue. He had shown his family that he could foot it in business and, proving the adage that 'money makes money' had continued to compile a considerable fortune through a mixture of solid calls and insightful investments. A pre-iPhone investment in Apple proved particularly 'fruitful' as his father liked to point out with agonising frequency.

Despite all this, he remained angry. The wealth meant nothing when he saw people he had played with and against featuring on the sports pages at movie premieres and on the cover of magazines. He wasn't totally sure that 'Mike and Dana's engagement ring drama' was his thing but it was a reminder of what he had been robbed of and another reminder that no one had been held accountable. He began to think of those who were enjoying the fame that he had been denied and those who had been directly involved in his injury. Life had been fine but as he tried to conceal his limp, the taunts of cruel young men were damaging. Young women who otherwise would have considered him quite a catch soon made their excuses as he shuffled his way to the bar or the bathroom. Maybe it was time to settle the score with those directly involved. Maybe it was time for some of those people to truly understand the price of fame.

36

Justin Ilesman enjoyed a party. Living in a large house in St Heliers, one of Auckland's most desirable suburbs, hosting was always on, particularly given his parents travelled frequently and his elder brother and sister were both at universities in other parts of the country. Ilesman hadn't quite got his head around university and was still a long way from full-time employment, choosing to fill his days running the till at the local wine shop.

A party for Ilesman didn't just mean a few beers with the boys. Beers were at the low end of a vast array of intoxicants and punters could be assured that their particular brand of escape was available in quantities ranging from personal use to commercial supply. His parents' spirits trolley was a showcase for all the top brands and parties would always require some 'perks from work' by way of replenishment.

This weekend promised to be a cracker. A day at the races would take them through until about four o'clock, then a cab through the 'burbs, a shower, throw on the smellies and the music, then ring Lisa Lloyd and make sure she brings at least a half dozen of her 'besties' – it would seriously damage his reputation to have an all-blokes affair.

And so it went. Several bottles of Moet watching the nags go around, a late trifecta to keep the score for the day around even and there they were as the sun began to fall at a rate slightly slower than the level of the litre bottle of Jack which dominated the huge outdoor table. The property was right on the edge of the cliffs above Gentleman's Bay with an envious view of Rangitoto and many of the other islands dotted around the Hauraki Gulf.

Ilesman was pleased with the way the night was progressing. A good smattering of mates from the footy club, a few rough types to provide cred and the sort of girls who would ensure dancing and spa-pool revelry was inevitable. Unfortunately, Ilesman had given everything he could get his hands on a red-hot go and was now beyond a normal description of inebriated. His last vestige of intelligence suggested he put his head down for a while but the effect was immediate and the party raged around him as he nodded off on one of the many loungers which dressed the deck.

When he woke, the night was cold and the music had died. The deck was empty and for all intents and purposes, the party was over. A yellow piece of paper was tucked under his arm and he immediately recognised the noise control warning document. *Nice one guys,* he thought as he cast a half-formed sweep around the debris. He sensed movement at the top of the stairs and tensed.

"Hey, Justin, how's it going?"

"Jesus, fucking hell. You scared the shit out of me. What are you still doing here?"

"Just arrived, mate. Heard these things kicked on forever but it's a pretty sad show."

"Yeah, I flaked pretty early and I think the cops must have shut it down. Even Lisa Lloyd pulled the pin."

"Well, since I'm here, let's have one for the road out by the cliff. It's a beautiful night."

"Fuck it, why not? Have a trawl through that chilly bin. Can't imagine they would have left any of the good stuff but there might be a couple of ice cold Steinies in there."

He fished around and, sure enough, there were a few remnants and indeed a couple of Steinlagers emerged from the watery ice.

"After you, mate."

Ilesman opened the gate that led to the cliff edge. They perched on the edge, swapping small talk about old school mates and asking with dubious sincerity, "What are you up to these days?"

The beers quickly drained and as they got up to leave, he took Ilesman gently by the shoulder.

"Justin, you know how I had that accident at footy training back at school?"

"Yeah, bit of a shocker for you."

"The thing is, I never really got the impression that you were sorry about causing that. You know it ruined my cricket career."

"Yeah, I heard about that," he said with a shrug.

"The problem I've got is that you sit around here having parties and getting on with your life. You're completely unaffected and I live with the accident forever. It doesn't seem fair to me."

"Well, mate, sometimes life isn't fair," he responded with all the wisdom of a drunken uncle.

He smiled. "Well, we agree on that Justin." Tightening his grip just a fraction, he motioned as if to bring Ilesman in for a hug but his intent was quite different as an airborne Ilesman discovered a millisecond later. The trip to the rocks below was brief and came to an end with a report like a wet beach towel being slapped against a surf club wall.

Vengeance was surprisingly easy.

37

He'd been following the surgeon for a while.

His research began quietly, assessing success rates where he could, mainly through word of mouth at sports clubs and speaking with players at rehabilitation centres and physios where he was a regular fixture. One afternoon, he was speaking to a member of the Auckland Rugby team, who asked him where he had gone for the surgery.

"I went to a guy called Max Lafarge. Know anything about him?"

The players' reaction was telling. "Jeez, bro, that might be part of the problem. We call him 'Max Lafactory' or 'Max Lafuckup.' Story is, he takes on too many patients and moves them through like a production line, gets tired, makes errors. He gets away with it because 'all injuries are different, no telling how you will react'." All the usual bullshit. None of the footy guys go to him anymore. We'd rather wait for 'Moose' Jensen or one of those guys to do the job.

He had always been prone to mood swings and his injury had not helped this failing. This news took him to a new place altogether and an old bat that had stayed in his boot was now being used to panel beat the rear right-hand door of his old Honda Civic. Had he known what was coming, Max Lafarge may have preferred to have been the car door.

38

He watched as Lafarge left his Remuera surgery in his late-model Audi coupe. Lafarge's habits followed a consistent rhythm. It was a short hop down Victoria Ave, then onto the waterfront and up Long Drive to his palatial Kohimaramara home, courtesy of the production line of patients. On a Wednesday he left his home for dinner and cards at the Northern Club and on Thursday, what he had discovered to be Lafarge's third wife left the house ostensibly for book club but as it happened turned out to be time at the Hyatt with a senior staff nurse from Southern Cross Hospital. Taking his wife in for Christmas drinks hadn't quite worked out as he'd imagined.

On this particular Thursday he waited for her BMW to flash past and walked stealthily as he could up the driveway. His knock was curt and demanding and Lafarge appeared quickly as if it was his wife having forgotten her book for another week. He'd never really twigged that her literary repertoire had not been enriched by her weekly club meetings.

"Coming, love."

"Oh, hello. Can I help you?"

"Dr Lafarge, you must not remember me. I was the cricketer you operated on. I thought I'd drop in and give you an update."

Lafarge gave him a quizzical look, then remembered that forgetting patients was ordinary form and recovered quickly.

"Yes, of course. How are you? I'm expecting guests but come in for a minute, it would be great to hear your news." His attempt at sincerity missed as he was about as interested in patients after they had paid as he was in his wife's clumsy attempts to run him through the night at book club.

"Please, have a seat. Can I get you a drink?"

"No, I'm good, thanks. I won't take much of your time."

"OK, I'll grab a gin if you don't mind. Tough day."

He walked over to his perfectly stocked drinks trolley, poured a lazy measure into a cut-crystal tumbler and sat down on the leather couch. "So tell me, how you are going?"

"Well, I just wanted to ask you a question first. I hear you operate on about 30% more patients a day than your peers, is that right?"

"I really wouldn't know about that but I do run an efficient ship if that's what you're getting at. A house like this doesn't come for nothing you know, and I've got to keep the wife in toys to say nothing of the payments for the other two."

Lafarge's jocular tone did nothing to quell the menace and the next question was as pointed.

"Of these operations, how many would you say you make mistakes in? You're only human after all."

"Mistakes? Well, I really don't know. I don't get sued very often if that's what you mean. Of course, there's going to be the odd operation that doesn't quite go to plan but what can you do?"

"What can you do indeed…how about fewer patients and a lot more care?"

"I'm not sure I need advice about how to run my practice. If you're not happy, there are avenues you can pursue. Now, if you don't mind, I've got a few things to attend to."

"Look before I go, can I just grab a quick glass of water?"

"Help yourself and pass me that gin bottle, if you wouldn't mind."

It wasn't that he misheard him but that the gin bottle was going to serve another purpose. As it cracked down on the back of his head, Lafarge barely had time to groan before he pitched forward and lay semi-conscious across the couch. He watched Lafarge for a moment, then reached into his jacket pocket, removing a sealed package. Tearing across the aluminium foil, he produced a shiny surgical instrument and held it up against the light. Leaning down, he grabbed Lafarge's hair and pulled his head back, revealing a pulsing vein on the side of his neck.

"Now, let's see who is a bit loose with the scalpel."

39

Mike Dunn ripped into his Chicken Tikka Masala with a vengeance. It seemed faintly ironic that after several weeks coping with foreign cuisine he would crave a curry on his return home. To be fair, the bangers and mash at the Ring of Bells also appealed but he did not regret this decision for a moment. He liked the way they added a bit of extra chilli to what is typically a mild dish and by the end of his onslaught, he had a bead on his upper lip and a drip on the end of his nose.

It was just after 7 pm, not an unreasonable time to reacquaint with Alpa Parekh. He felt strangely nervous but chided himself, given they had spent such a short time in each other's company and none of that truly alone.

"Alpa, hi, it's Mike Dunn."

"Mike, how are you?" Mike felt a short surge of pleasure at her enthusiastic tone.

"I'm great but as you may have read, things have been a bit grim on the work front. Sorry, I haven't called until now but I'd love to catch up again."

"Don't apologise. If the papers are anything to go by, you've had a bit on. When did you have in mind?"

"What about some lunch over the weekend? I know a great pub up near you – have you been to The Chequers?"

"No I haven't but it'll have to be Sunday. I've agreed to go to lunch at Crispin's parents on Saturday."

Dunn couldn't have felt more deflated if he'd ridden a bicycle over a fakir's bed. It wasn't so bad that she had a boyfriend but he'd completely misjudged her if she felt Crispin was a sound moniker.

Alpa filled Dunn's unintentional silence. "Crispin's father and my father were at Cambridge together. Dad wanted me to go and pay my respects and Crispin's harmless enough but so not my type." Her use of 'so' amused Dunn as much as her explanation delighted him.

Well, that's great, Alpa. I'll pick you up outside Ede and Ravenscroft on Sunday, about 11?"

"That would be lovely, Mike. I'll see you then. Let's make sure we eat this time! Oh, I must tell you. I overheard a conversation in a bar a week or so back and thought you would be interested."

"Oh, yes, go on."

"I was with a friend of mine in Kolkata and some cricketers pulled in alongside us at the bar. One of them sounded like he was trying to recruit players to. Well, he said they would be rewarded handsomely for doing unusual things on the cricket field. I know that's vague but it sounded bloody dodgy."

"Bloody hell, it sure does. I don't suppose you heard a name?"

"Actually, I did. The guy doing all the talking was the Pakistani opener. Does the name Faisal Shaikh set off any alarm bells for you?"

"Unfortunately, it does, Alpa. Let's add that to the list for Chequers."

"OK, see you Sunday."

Dunn put down the phone, delighted to have found Alpa again and doubly delighted that she remained as single as he and apparently looking forward to meeting again. He was also fascinated to hear more on Faisal Shaikh. The bastard is still knee-deep in match fixing by the sound of things and he may not be out of the woods on the murders either.

With a restrained punch of the air, he went to his stereo, put on David Gray's 'White Ladder' and settled down to go through his notes again. The more he looked at it, the more he realised he was looking for a vengeful individual – these were crimes of hatred, not just random acts of violence. Collectively, these cricketers represented something that the killer either aspired to or detested. Had they in some way taken something from him that he believed was his?

Friday night I'm going nowhere, all the lights are changing green to red, the music seemed to mock him as he worked through the scribblings and jottings of a hundred interviews and a thousand thoughts. The phone rang and Mike followed the ringtone out to the kitchen. Simon Feast was on the other end.

"Mike, no big deal, I don't think but Andy Beaumont hasn't made it to Derby yet. Apparently, he's phoned through to say he's got a touch of flu but he'll be up first thing in the morning."

"Thanks, Feasty, I appreciate you letting me know." Dunn was tempted just to carry on with his work but with Beaumont living in Fulham, it was a short trip and an ideal opportunity to have a quiet yarn about what had been happening.

Dunn reversed his trusty old Audi onto the road and headed off to Beaumont's house. The warm temperature had attracted many out into London's evening and progress was slow down the Old Brompton Road. Anticipating a rugged-up Beaumont at home, Dunn drove patiently and as he approached Beaumont's address, a sports car hurtled out onto the road, about 50 metres ahead of him. The clear evening afforded a good sighting of the registration, a personalised plate, which was not surprising given the nature of the vehicle. 'PEPPY' was all it read and Dunn was about to ignore it when he realised the car had been extremely close to number 16 before it began its urban rally. He parked his car and rang through to Jolian Ford-Robertson, whose warp speed data searches and analytical brilliance had cemented him a place on the team.

"Jolian, I was hoping you could help me with something," asked Dunn in a manner which implied a choice that both knew didn't exist. "Get me the ownership details on a license plate 'PEPPY'. Papa – Echo – Papa – Papa – Yankee. Good man." Dunn clicked off and walked purposefully toward Andy Beaumont's front door. It was with some discomfort that he noted that the door was not closed but perhaps the sports car driver had left the house at the same speed they had left the curb.

"Andy," called Dunn. "It's Mike Dunn here. I'm an investigator with the ICC. You might recall we met during the match fixing investigations. Do you mind if I come up?"

An open door combined with no reply was a disturbing combination but as Dunn climbed the stairs, he could see no evidence of a struggle, although a broken heel from a woman's shoe greeted him at the top of the stairs. Dunn slowed completely and moved warily into the living area.

"Andy, are you here?"

Still no reply meant either Andy Beaumont was fast asleep or, given recent history, he might just be in a spot of bother. A few empty cans of Stella were sitting on the coffee table and, with all the usual accoutrements of the modern home, all looked rather normal. However, as he rounded the gap into the kitchen, it was clear things were far from normal for Andy Beaumont.

40

Trinnick and Dunn looked down on Beaumont's body, slumped against his dishwasher. A close-up would suggest an inebriated man passed out in his kitchen but a wider shot would reveal a vast pool of blood, suggesting death delivered by something sharp enough to play havoc with all manner of arteries. Beaumont's replica Chelsea shirt hardly looked damaged apart from a hole in one of the letters of the sponsor's logo. Suffice to say, the effect on Andy Beaumont was disproportionate and the pathologist suggested it had taken only a few moments for the hole in his heart to end his life.

"If there is a positive note to this, sir, it's that at last we have a clean crime scene. I've kept everyone apart from the forensic team well away from the house."

"Talk me through it, Mike. We've got a fit young guy here. How does he get killed in his own kitchen without the merest sign of a struggle?"

"The front door is in perfectly good nick, so the killer either sneaked into the house as you allude or was welcomed in. Either way, there has been no struggle, nothing knocked over and no breakages. Looking at the empty beer cans, I'd conclude that Beaumont was enjoying a drink with his visitor when they've come in close to one and other and the killer has put some sort of sharp object through his ribs. To get that close, there must be some sort of intimacy, a cuddle or an arm around the shoulders. Either way, it's pretty clear Beaumont had no idea what was coming."

"You mentioned a theory this afternoon about some kind of righteous crusader. Was Beaumont on your list of potential targets?"

Outwardly, Dunn gave nothing away. Inside, he was in worse shape than Andy Beaumont. "I'm sorry to admit, sir, that yes, he was. I tried to call but couldn't get on to him. I thought he would be up at Derby with his teammates and I asked an old colleague to keep a watch over him. As soon as I heard he was still in London, I came over. Obviously, I was too late."

Trinnick pondered this response and Dunn braced himself for the inevitable and, in hindsight, deserved dressing down. He was relieved that Alan Norton, the head of the forensic team, appeared in the kitchen. Norton was a veteran of many years of crime scenes and it took a lot to shake his indifference to death. Andy Beaumont was just another victim to process for the rotund, dishevelled man with Coke-bottle spectacles.

"We've covered the house. No evidence of forced entry. DNA samples taken from sexual activity in the bedroom and the outline of a woman's buttocks on the outside of the shower."

Dunn's mouth suggested a hint of a grin at Alan Norton's deadpan delivery but he feared he was the only one who considered this find to be even remotely amusing.

Trinnick stomped on the mood like a farmer despatching a fleeing field mouse. "Hate to bring it to your attention, Mike, but a man is dead in the kitchen – a man you might easily have saved had you been a little more on the ball."

"Yes, sorry, sir. Alan, what are your thoughts on the cause of death?"

"From what I can tell, Beaumont's been skewered. We'll have to wait for the coroner but my money would be on a single blow piercing the heart. A skewer or something similar would be the only weapon that would do so much damage from such a minimal entry wound. A couple of other interesting things – the heel from a pair of Jimmy Choo shoes was at the top of the stairs and a book was open on the coffee table. The piece of shoe was no doubt from a woman but the book is intriguing. It's the souvenir programme from the World Youth tournament Beaumont played in. Not the sort of book you'd have out all the time and highly unlikely to be the sort of material you'd thumb through with a lady. Even I'd come up with something more imaginative than that," added Norton.

Given the chance, I bet you would, thought Dunn, rapidly revising his opinion of the bespectacled forensic.

"Sir, I saw a late-model Porsche Macan leaving just as I arrived. The Jimmy Choo shoes would fit that sort of profile perfectly. She was in one hell of a hurry but I did manage to note her registration plate."

"Good, Mike. Who owns the car then?"

Dunn was about to embark on the dreaded 'not sure yet' response when his phone rang.

"Jolian here, sir. I've found out a bit more about your speedster."

"Good stuff, Jolian. Tell me more."

"The car was a black Porsche and I must say I'm surprised you didn't notice that. They're very distinctive, particularly the new shape."

"Thanks, Jolian, but I'm not a train spotter when it comes to cars. Just let me know who owns it."

"The current owner is a name you will know well. It's registered to Timothy Faxon-Jones but we both know it is highly unlikely he was behind the wheel."

Dunn was slightly miffed that he hadn't made the connection from the personalised plate 'PEPPY'. Melanie Faxon-Jones had often used her maiden name of Pepper and her black Porsche had featured in a Daily Express photo montage entitled 'Just who do you think you are?' after numerous acts of illegal parking outside London clubs and restaurants.

Tracking down Melanie Faxon-Jones did not require a nationwide search. Dunn appeared at her Knightsbridge apartment where a cautious voice responded on the intercom.

"Hello?"

"Mrs Faxon-Jones?"

"Yes?"

"Mrs Faxon-Jones, it's Mike Dunn here, I'm an investigator with the ICC. I'd like to talk to you about Andy Beaumont."

"What about him? I know who he is, of course, having been in the team with Tim but I didn't know him that well."

Dunn felt like putting a shoulder to the door as he had no appetite for this little dance.

"Didn't know him, Mrs Faxon-Jones?"

"Didn't, don't, whatever."

Dunn was tiring of communicating with a small black grill.

"Mrs Faxon-Jones, you were seen leaving his flat earlier this afternoon. Let's drop the act, shall we? Let me come up and discuss this face to face." He was about to throw in the time honoured. "Or perhaps you would prefer to accompany me to the station." When the door clicked and Dunn found himself in the lobby.

Moments later, the lift arrived and Melanie appeared, brandishing a security card.

"No one gets in without one of these, not even you lot."

Dunn proffered his hand to the jeans and T-shirt clad woman. A combination of tears and Bombay Sapphire had left her with a bleariness that rendered her unrecognisable from the social pages' spreads.

They entered the lift and she hit PH. Arriving at the top floor, he felt he had walked into a Sotheby's real-estate shoot. Dunn didn't know his armoires from his chiffoniers but he was certain the Faxon-Joneses didn't get their furniture from Ikea. An anachronistic grandfather clock added a certain elegance to the décor while modern and classical works adorned the walls.

"Mrs Faxon-Jones," began Dunn. "I saw you leaving Andy Beaumont's this afternoon. You may or may not know that Mr Beaumont is dead. For the moment, you head our suspect list unless, of course, you can give us reason to alter that view."

Melanie Faxon-Jones beckoned to Dunn to take a seat and proceeded to light a cigarette as she sat down on the large leather sofa that dominated the living area.

"I'll tell you what I saw but there's no way Tim's parents can know of this. One of the provisions of his will precludes any extra-marital activity. I'd be left with nothing and God knows I deserve more than that after putting up with him for so long."

Dunn viewed her impassively. "I'm not sure you're in a great bargaining position here. Tell me your version of events, leave nothing out and we'll take it from there. I'm only interested in finding a murderer. Why you were at Beaumont's yesterday and why you were in such a hurry to leave?"

"When I see my lover lying in a pool of blood, I'm not of a mind to stick around and meet the killer. I walked in, saw him on the kitchen floor and scarpered. I was terrified."

"You didn't think to call the police? An ambulance?"

"There's no way I could afford to get caught there. Imagine the delight the press would have with it. It seemed pretty obvious there was nothing I could do for Andy. After that, it was every man for himself, so to speak."

Dunn was amazed at the callousness with which she rationalised the situation. He was also convinced that, although she was there, it was unlikely she would have had the strength or the motivation to murder Andy Beaumont.

"Did you see anyone on the street as you arrived or on the way out?"

She exhaled deeply, leaving a trail of smoke drifting across the room. "I was petrified, Mr Dunn. I just floored it out of there as soon as I could. Knackered a perfectly good pair of shoes in the process."

Dunn got up to leave. He didn't enjoy this woman's company and was sure she had little to add. As was his habit, he handed his card to Faxon-Jones. "If you think of anything else."

They walked back to the door and she summoned the lift. As he moved to enter, she grabbed his arm.

"Wait on, I did see one thing that looked a bit odd. There was a bloke in a suit around the corner on Fulham Palace Road. He hailed a cab and as he ran across the road in front of me, he moved like an old man. For a fit-looking bloke, he had a hell of a limp."

41

Dunn returned to Beaumont's flat and picked his way carefully through the lounge area. Experts had combed the scene with their usual vigilance but Dunn couldn't avoid a feeling that there was something there that could link them to the killer. He visualised a man walking up the stairs, shaking hands and sitting down for a beer or two. What had passed between them? More importantly, what had made Beaumont's death necessary? The beer cans had been returned to the lab for forensic examination in the hope that some DNA might be left in the dregs but other than that, a mass of fingerprint dusting was all that remained to corral evidence.

Dunn made his way into the kitchen but apart from enough O-positive to keep Great Ormond Street in plasma, it was clear that there was little interaction in there. No dishes, no bottles and little evidence that anyone but Beaumont has spent much time there. Returning to the couches, he grabbed the cricket programme that had been sitting on the coffee table and had a bit of a thumb through. As a cricket fan, he was always interested in old publications and became quite engrossed. The incongruity of tobacco sponsorship in an age group tournament programme was amusing but the turning of the next page removed his grin abruptly. Staring back at him in full colour – and in full health – was a young Pradip Mistry, profiled as a future star of world cricket. A few pages later, the pudgy visage of privilege sneered up at him – none other than a youthful Timothy Faxon-Jones. It came as no surprise that a couple of handsome West Indians appeared soon after. By now, Dunn was taking stairs in twos.

At Jermyn St, Gordon Landolfi and Lucinda Wright were trying to piece together the trail of death, hoping to have something to offer Dunn when he got back to the office, whenever that might be.

Landolfi, always cheerful and ever the optimist, spoke first. "I think we might have been on the right track, Lu. We certainly picked the victim and if we've got the motivation right, perhaps this spree is over."

"That would be nice in some respects, Gordy. It certainly doesn't help the victims but it might help a few cricketers sleep better at night. Problem is, I was thinking about this yesterday and the whole Se7en imitation, righteous crusade thing just doesn't sit well."

Landolfi had been quite keen on the Se7en theory and was about to protest when Dunn burst through the door, forehead dripping with sweat and with what looked like an old sports programme in his hand.

"I'm with you on that, Lu," Dunn replied. "I think there might be something afoot beyond that theory. I've thought about the players involved countless times in the last month and I couldn't link them together – but have a look through that programme and tell me what you see."

Wright grabbed the programme and in less than a minute looked up at Dunn. "You're kidding me."

"Sadly, not, Lu. Weird as it sounds. I think the killer is building a World XI."

Landolfi fired a whiteboard marker across the table. "Oh, Jesus. Bloody hell. Lu, write the names up again."

As she did so, it was clear the theory had legs. She wrote the numerals 1–11 down the left-hand side of the whiteboard, filling in the names against probable spots in the batting order. There were no double-ups.

"Lu, at the back of the programme are the names of all the players, by team, of the eight countries involved. Check it for me again but I'm almost certain all our victims are listed."

It took but a moment for Wright to confirm. "This is scary, Mike, not just because you are probably onto something but it means this guy is far from finished."

Dunn took charge. "OK, let's look at this. If I'm going to murder a World XI, who would I pick from here? I've already got numbers three, four and maybe six in the batting order. I've got my opening bowlers and I've got a wicket keeper. In theory, that leaves me with a third quick, a spinner, maybe an all-rounder and three more batsmen. If this person is indeed 'picking' a World XI, which players are in the most danger?"

Although 'armchair teams' are picked in pubs most nights, for everything from 'worst Test team ever' to 'best team with names more than nine letters long' (which always favoured the Sri Lankans), he felt they had a good handle on who the world's best players were. In certain situations, the player was without peer, in others there were numerous options. After some deliberation they came up with:

Seam Bowler – Morne Kruger, South Africa

Opening Batsmen – Rob DeBeer, South Africa and Faisal Shaikh, Pakistan

Spinner – Gareth Wickramysinghe, Sri Lankan

All-Rounder – Cam Peters, New Zealand

Middle-Order Batsman – Abishek Misra, India, Chris Wilks, Australia, Pieter van Zyl, South African but not currently available.

"Check this against the programme. Are all these players mentioned?"

Landolfi looked up from his tablet. "I can do better than that, Mike. I've just googled the tournament team they select at the end of the competition. It's pretty much what we've got on the whiteboard, all bar Peters, the New Zealander."

"Who's the all-rounder in the team if it's not Peters?"

"A guy by the name of Marty Fowler."

"Never heard of him. Do some research and see what he did after his moment of fame."

Dunn considered his list. There must be some way of telling these guys to exercise caution without alarming them or having this half-baked but instinctively correct theory splashed across the press.

"We've got the Melanie Faxon-Jones description, which matches the other sighting of this guy. It was too much of a co-incidence that the 'limping man' would appear near two of the murders."

The suit, the limp, the athletic appearance. Dunn had no doubt that his killer was in England. At least, Dunn thought, according to his reckoning, there were no more 'murder candidates' in the England team and he could start to construct a protective web around the others on his list.

Dunn was keen on a coffee, so he offered to do the honours for the team and suggested they take fifteen before reconvening. He strode down Jermyn St, looking for a spot where he could map out his plan of attack. Having ordered the coffees and the standing order of a cannoli for Landolfi, Dunn took a deep breath and thought it through. He had two tasks – work out a way to apprehend the killer and try to keep the world's cricketers safe as he did so. Obviously success with the first task guaranteed the second but Dunn knew that he had no way of knowing in which part of the globe this maniac would strike next. It was the back page of the *Daily Mail* that gave him his first steer but instead of providing encouragement, it chilled him to the core.

South Africans arrive confident of victory read the headline.

"Jesus!" he exclaimed, leaving traces of coffee staining the story. "He's sticking around to take care of any South Africans that might make his 'XI'."

Dunn was embarrassed that he hadn't considered such an obvious move but, to be fair, the World XI theory had only just landed. Mentally, he was already on a plane around the world to protect Pakistanis and Sri Lankans when, by all reckoning, the killer had figured on 'easy pickings' without the inconvenience of international customs and the now-alerted Interpol.

Dunn dialled the secretary of the ICC to get details of where the South Africans and specifically Morne Kruger and Rob De Beer could be reached. If they were in London and he had every reason to believe this was so, he needed to put a decent security net around the team. With terrorism an on-going issue, it would not be difficult to justify strong security around a touring team in London without having myriad conspiracy theorists speculating about an 'increased police presence'.

"Mike Dunn here. Just wanting to get contact details for the South Africans. I assume they are in London?"

"Indeed they are, Mr Dunn," replied Cathy Jacobs with the resentment of one who had been interrupted from her morning cuppa and a stint on Candy Crush. Her addiction to the game had taken strong hold and any distractions were extremely unwelcome.

"They're at the Grosvenor. I'll give you Garth Kirsten's number too. As manager, he will know all the scheduled movements of the team."

Dunn jotted it down and thanked her just before the click of a terminated connection.

"You have a good day too, love," he muttered sarcastically.

The phone rang once before Landolfi answered. "Gordy, the South Africans arrived in town last night. If we're running with the World XI theory, there are a couple of potential victims on that list. You guys carry on, I'm off to their hotel to let them know."

42

Guy Trinnick often enjoyed breakfast at Grangers in Notting Hill. He'd heard it was an Australian venture but its combination of breakfast options and friendly staff made it a more than agreeable spot to start the day. In addition, it was usually busy, which allowed for a nice degree of anonymity – just another diner with his head buried in *The Times*, enjoying a cup of tea and a boiled egg with toast, always cut into soldiers. He took a sip of his tea and began to embark on the crossword which is nearly as famous as the masthead. As he did so, a man assumed the seat opposite him and greeted him cordially.

"Good morning, Mr Trinnick."

"Hello. I'm not sure I know you and if you wish to speak to me, perhaps you'd be good enough to make an appointment." Trinnick was not one for the impromptu and for him, 'shooting the breeze' was as absurd as it sounded.

"Yes, I could do that but I imagine you'd be keen on a chat. It's about the cricketers."

Trinnick eyed the man cautiously. As far as the public were concerned, the deaths of the cricketers were random unconnected acts. No one had linked them together in a way that would lead to them being referred to collectively.

"Who are you and what exactly are you referring to?"

"I'm referring to the murders of a number of the world's finest cricketers, a case which you and Mike Dunn are making no progress in solving."

Trinnick viewed his impromptu breakfast guest with a look just short of disdain. "If you have something official to say, I need you to come to my office and make a statement. I'm happy to hear your thoughts if you believe you have something that will lead us to the killer but I'm not going to discuss it here."

"Well, Mr Trinnick, it's not quite like that. Let's just say it's me that needs some help and you're going to provide it."

Trinnick felt an immediate sense of unease as the conversation took an unusual turn.

"What do you mean 'help you'?"

"I'm the person you're looking for and I'm not finished yet. I will be travelling farther afield and it will not serve my purpose to be stopped at immigration for any reason. I believe you can help with this, given your connections with the various agencies."

Trinnick contemplated a lunge and an attempt to incapacitate but his quarry revealed a strong body beneath a tight-fitting T-shirt, his biceps resembling grapefruit and his chest like a sports-shop mannequin – one on one, this was not his to win.

"I can't help you with that. Even if I wanted to, it is just too impractical." He glanced around the restaurant, desperately hoping that a raised eyebrow would bring one of the wait staff over.

"You can and you will, otherwise I might be forced to share some information that would end your career and, frankly, would end you."

"What are you talking about? I live alone, I work for the ICC and I collect stamps. I'm not sure that a passion for First Day Covers is particularly newsworthy." Trinnick was feeling quite proud. He was not a gifted raconteur and felt he had taken the upper hand. His hubris was short lived as a card from a woman named Brandi was placed in the shell of his boiled egg.

"I'm sure Brandi's particularly creative offerings would indeed be newsworthy, Mr Trinnick. I'm sure your board, your colleagues and the journos at *The Sun* would find it all fascinating."

"This is ridiculous. You come in here, interrupt my breakfast and give me a card that could have been found pinned on the side of a lamppost and expect that I'll just crumble and acquiesce? I'm sorry but if that is your leverage, I'll be on my way."

He motioned to leave but quickly felt the table pushed firmly against his paunch. A phone was being proffered.

"Would you like to listen to this up close or shall I put it on speaker?"

"This is preposterous. What have you got here, a recorded message which would be totally inadmissible and virtually impossible to substantiate."

His tirade stopped as rapidly as it had begun as he heard Brandi's voice outlining in granular detail the events of the previous night and her gratitude for his regular patronage. It was clear he was dealing with a man of considerable resource and persuasion. Trinnick knew that his career ambitions were going to hit something of a brick wall if he didn't find a way to navigate this. His current profile of the quintessential 'safe pair of hands' would be destroyed and no senior official could enjoy promotion with even the merest hint of a scandal permeating around him.

"Be specific, then. Tell me exactly what you need, Mr…"
"Nice try but you don't need my name for now. It sounds like we're starting to get on the same page, Mr Trinnick. I don't expect to hear from you and you certainly won't be hearing from me apart to advise when and where I need access. Just make sure that I'm free to pass through any borders I choose and you and Brandi can stay as loved up and lewd as you like. Good day, Mr Trinnick."

Trinnick watched him leave the building and head down Westbourne Grove. This was not a situation his wildest dream would have realised and he knew he had a choice to make. Remain silent, save his job and leave this apparently normal but clearly deranged man to continue his 'crusade' or reveal all and end his career in a single sentence. He looked at the clues on the crossword, but nothing would come to him.

43

Sitting in the lobby of the Grosvenor Hotel, he reflected on the previous month's activities. Having been in four countries and crossed myriad time zones, he was a tad jaded and a little on the prickly side – not good news for his next subject. It wasn't that he was particularly vindictive in his work but he did have standards.

He had been brought up in the implied privilege of middle class in the suburb of Ponsonby, a chameleon of a postcode in Auckland, New Zealand's largest city. It was a suburb that went from fine dining at one end of the strip to poetry readings at the Gluepot Tavern at the other. Advertising executives lived within audible distance of O'Connell St lawyers, who in turn neighboured alternative life stylers rusted on to a '70s' vibe.

As the second son of a family anchored firmly in society's central stratum – Dad, an insurance broker, Mum, a primary school teacher – he always felt mildly claustrophobic. Every glance into the future suggested the life of an ordinary man and the mortgage, wife, two kids and a dachshund scenario chilled him to the bone. A promising cricket career had been ended abruptly by injury, necessitating other paths be forged.

Not surprisingly, an opportunity to move to Melbourne was taken with a speed usually reserved for those with differences of opinions on matters of law. His early work was unrewarding, coming as it did on the whim of his editor, an over fed and under educated man, who unfortunately had just enough Murdoch connections to preside over a group of writers who were his intellectual and literary superiors. Noel Fenton's editorial process would involve doling out assignments in a manner which can only be described as opportunistic – the greater the opportunity for sexual relations with the writer, the higher profile the leads were. It hadn't occurred to Fenton that he had more chance of winning a Pulitzer than luring one of his charges to the bedroom and yet he persisted, assigning young women to politicians, rock stars and sporting scandals, while male staffers covered council by-elections and Mrs Jones' talking alpaca.

Despite such barriers, eventually talent shone through. One of Fenton's 'usual suspects', a feisty and free-spirited journo by the name of Deborah Bracken was assigned to write a feature on a future cricketing superstar by the name of Mitchell Howard. Despite Bracken's professionalism and acceptance of the fact that immediate career advancement was in the hands – quite literally – of 'Fingers Fenton', this was a gig she was desperate to avoid. Sport was subject she had a care factor of nil for and she saw sports journalism as a refuge for the vicarious. Frankly, she would rather profile a Terence Trent D'Arby tribute act than have anything to do with cricket and cricketers.

Deborah Bracken was not short on persuasive power and it took only a fraction of it to get the young Kiwi to visit Howard. He would write the story, she would get the by-line and Fingers would be none the wiser. She would also owe him one, never a bad thing in a world where information is the gold standard.

Howard proved to be an elusive interviewee and less than friendly to the young journalist. Half an hour of mono – tone and syllable – left the writer with several gaps to fill and a feeling that they would do this again in the future, depending on his response to the story. That said, the likelihood of Howard reading it was contingent on him putting his bat down for half an hour which for the moment seemed a distant possibility.

Bracken's plan was going perfectly until the sub editor, who had been clearly briefed but was a tad forgetful, sent the copy through for editorial review having amended punctuation and grammar but not the author's name. 'Fingers' was furious but as he absorbed the first few lines he could not help but acknowledge the quality of the work – and quickly realised he could claim this as part of his talent development process at his next performance review.

Many years of insightful and occasional dismemberment of his subjects later, he sat ready for his next assault. As had become customary, his quarry was late, so he approached the receptionist, who smiled encouragingly.

"Morning, love, can you ring a room for me? I'm looking for Morne Kruger. The name's Mellem, Frank Mellem."

44

The South African cricket team lounged in various poses in front of the television in Garth Kirsten's suite. They had gathered to watch the rugby international between New Zealand and their beloved Springboks, live from Christchurch. The time change from New Zealand meant the game was being played in the morning local time – an ideal opportunity for the boys to get together and relax prior to the hard day's training ahead.

Morne Kruger at 190 cm and 105 kg's, dominated the seating at the centre of the screen. As a senior player and a former Junior Springbok, his interest in the game was more acute than most. Many of the players in the team would have preferred football but they were loath to proffer this preference while the Boks were in action. It was tantamount to treason to Morne Kruger, who made every break and crashed into every tackle with his rugby heroes. It had been suggested that Kruger would have swapped all his 102 caps for the South African cricket team for just one opportunity to lead the Boks on to the stadium formerly known as Ellis Park for a test match against the All Blacks.

Unfortunately, Christchurch was something of a graveyard for touring sides, often turning on weather that would make a Siberian grimace and today's match was no exception. As the players trooped off to training, they knew that Kruger's mood had darkened and they could expect a lively net session while he worked out his frustration.

As the last of the players filed out of Kirsten's door, the phone rang.

"Carry on, guys. It's probably just the press. Sort out the gear and the coach and I'll see you all down at the lobby."

Garth Kirsten was often in demand with the press. As South Africa's only true world class all-rounder in the post-apartheid years, he had been a driving force in re-establishing the credibility of South African cricket. His performances with bat and ball spoke for themselves but Kirsten added more than that. A marvellous communicator, he bridged the gap between the two South Africa's and gave all South Africans a player and a man to respect. After a brief spell in business after his playing days, Kirsten returned to the fold and was soon appointed manager of the South African team. Genial and easy going, the press respected his views on the game and Kirsten appreciated that his availability did much for the image of his team and of cricket.

Before grabbing the phone, he looked for his iPad containing all his player information, tour dates and the like. The last thing he wanted was to be misquoted about the team or make a commitment he couldn't meet. The iPad was his Bible and if ever the team wanted to induce sweaty-palmed panic in their manager, sequestering his tablet was the way to go.

"Thank God for that!" he exclaimed as he saw the corner of the device winking at him from under the couch. "Nice try, you bastards," he remarked to any of his team who might have still been present but none had remained to enjoy the manager's momentary discomfort. As he got to his feet, he heard the door to his room close. Swivelling around, he expected to see one of the guys collecting a forgotten item. A set of ear buds, a room key or the seemingly permanent adornment that sunglasses had become, were always being left in team rooms, on buses and other places that required a little more explanation. This time, though, there was no one from the team and instead he saw a man in a hotel uniform with a curiously amused grin on his face.

45

It was a relieved Mike Dunn, who spied Morne Kruger, lounging in the lobby of the Grosvenor. Surrounded by his teammates and engrossed in conversation, he was the healthiest-looking cricketer he had seen in some time, frankly. Dunn entered the hotel and went immediately to Kruger's group. He was pleased to see a couple of plain-clothes policemen in the vicinity and felt that he might at last be getting in front of whomever his nemesis was.

"Morne, my name is Mike Dunn. I'm with the ICC."

"I know who you are, Mr Dunn. You put a couple of my teammates out to pasture for being dumb enough to try and fix matches."

"So I did." He paused, not knowing where Kruger stood on this.

Kruger's response brought considerable relief. "They were bloody stupid and they've learnt their lesson. Anyway, what can I do for you? I thought the game was pretty clean these days."

"Unfortunately, there are those that will always be trying to create a market but there's something else I want to talk to you about. Do you mind wandering over to the restaurant?"

"No problem but the bus leaves in five."

"I won't need any more than that," he replied as he motioned toward a spare table. "Morne, you will be aware that some of your better performed opponents have been murdered lately."

"Yes, bloody shocking. Good blokes most of them, too, especially those West Indian boys."

"We aren't sure of the motive or if there is any connection," Dunn continued carefully. "But one theory is that some madman is building a World XI. All the players murdered to date would walk into a World XI and I'd have to put you in that category as well. I'm just saying that you need to be extra careful. We'll have men keeping watch but just make sure you keep company until we know something more."

Kruger looked stunned. "Wow, I hadn't looked at things that way. I'll certainly be careful but we've got a test series to win here. I can't go into my shell on your hunch alone."

"No, I understand that. I just wanted to let you know and I do believe you need to be extra careful. Andy Beaumont was found murdered yesterday and he too could be considered a likely starter for a World XI. We think you and Rob De Beer are the most likely candidates from South Africa."

"Bloody hell, this is getting weird. OK, I'll keep my head down and stay with the boys as much as possible. But two Poms in a World XI? It doesn't help your theory."

Dunn walked back across the lobby. He wasn't sure whether Kruger was being humorous or just displaying the directness that many South Africans are known for. Either way, he was pleased to have delivered his message and it seemed to sink home.

Dunn wanted to catch up with Garth Kirsten while he was in the hotel. It was important that he establish contact with the team manager and let him know some of the detail that he had given Kruger. He wasn't going to give him the full World XI theory but the fact that international cricketers were being killed at an increasing rate suggested he would be remiss in not providing something to the manager about two players who were clearly at risk.

"Guys," said Dunn to no one in particular. "Is Garth Kirsten about?"

"Probably looking for his iPad." Offered one of them, eliciting guffaws for reasons not readily apparent to Dunn. "He took a call just as we were leaving his room – we'd been up there watching the rugby – that was 20 odd minutes ago though. It's not like Garth to give a long interview off the cuff. Why don't you get reception to call his room?"

"Good thought," responded Dunn and walked over to the reception desk. A queue of business travellers had formed and Dunn found himself fourth in line. After what seemed an age but was probably ten minutes, Dunn was face to face with a receptionist whose smile was about as sincere as The Joker's.

"Good morning, could you put me through to Mr Kirsten's room, please." The flash of his badge helped avoid the usual rigmarole.

"No answer there, sir. Is it urgent?"

Dunn was about to answer 'No' but decided against it. "As a matter of fact, I need to get in touch as soon as possible."

"Fine, sir. I'll have one of the bell staff go to his room."

Mathew Fagley hopped into the lift and headed up to Garth Kirsten's room. *Bloody nice not to have to lug bags up for a change*, he thought.

The chime indicated he had hit the top floor and he walked down the corridor to get Mr Kirsten. Knocking tentatively, he called out, "Mr Kirsten, hotel staff here. Just checking you are OK. You have a visitor in the lobby." After a couple more knocks at increased volume, Mathew Fagley thought a little look around the manager's suite wouldn't do any harm. After all, he'd been asked to go and get him, so it was only being thorough.

Slipping the card into the lock, he carefully pushed the door open. "Mr Kirsten, are you there?" He contemplated a look through the gear and playing strips but the last thing he wanted was to be in mid-rummage and have him storm out of the bath with his headphones on. The room appeared empty though, so Fagley grabbed a bat and played a couple of imaginary shots. He eased past the kitchen and slipped a packet of Planters nuts in his pocket. Entering the bedroom, he noticed that the bathroom door was pulled but not closed and he froze, thinking that, sure enough, Mr Kirsten was going to come out of the bathroom and see him standing there with a bat in his hands and a packet of nuts protruding from his blazer pocket.

Feeling he was at the point of no return, he eased the bathroom door open. His speed out of the suite over the first few metres was extraordinary and given that taking the lift meant he would have to stop, he opted for the stairs. Around and around he went until emerging in the lobby, exhausted. His training (and the discretion that was supposed to go with it) had passed from his mind on about the eighth flight of stairs and he blurted to anyone who could hear, "Mr Kirsten...he's lying in his bath! I think he's dead!"

Dunn shoved Fagley into the lift and frantically pushed at the buttons to return to Kirsten's floor. Sprinting down the corridor with an exhausted Fagley close behind, he yelled at the young bellhop. "Get this bloody door open!"

"Yes, sir," Fagley heaved. Poking his security card at the slot in the door, Fagley took several goes before getting the green light. Dunn shouldered his way into the suite.

Dunn pivoted left and immediately saw why Fagley had bolted. Kirsten was indeed lying in his bath, bathing more in blood than water, arms splayed like a child's doll and looking about as lifelike. The water was running but Kirsten was fully clothed, suggesting an early soak had not been part of his plan for the morning.

Dunn couldn't be sure he was dead and grabbed at pulse points. His paramedic training was a distant memory but he was sure he could feel something from Kirsten's neck.

"Call an ambulance, lad!" he yelled in a tone which caused a frantic Fagley to stab at the keypad, grateful he wasn't required to form a sentence.

Dunn did his best to put Kirsten in the recovery position but was reluctant to move him. The blood seemed to have poured from the back of his head, so either the fall into the bath or a blow from behind was the likely cause. Either way, Garth Kirsten may have been the first person to evade death in what was becoming an almost futile pursuit.

Fagley looked down beside the bed and saw what was the most likely cause of Kirsten's discomfort. A cricket stump, replete with blood and woven with hair lay beside the manager's bed.

"Sir, I think I've found the weapon," he said and bent down to pick it up.

"Leave it!" screamed Dunn and moved the distraught bell hop to one side. Sure enough the weapon had every hallmark of an inflictor of blunt force trauma and Dunn, although mindful of Kirsten's plight hoped there might be something here that would add to the meagre amount of trace they had to work with.

"What's your name, lad?"

"Mathew Fagley, sir."

"Sorry to yell at you, Mathew. I'm Mike Dunn. Well done on your quick response, but now I'd like you to head back down to the lobby and wait for me there. We'll have a chat about what you saw after the paramedics get here."

Fagley was only too pleased to exit and Dunn was left to ponder another tangent in this caper. What did Kirsten have to do with building a World XI? Maybe there's something else he was missing? Dunn glanced out over Hyde Park as a growing despair formed in his gut. *I'm no closer to this guy than I was after Mistry.*

46

This one is going to bring me more pleasure than all the others combined, he thought, as he observed his quarry. Some of the victims were necessary evils given his plan, but this guy was mocking everything that the killer had aspired to. There was no doubt he was among the world's best but he showed no appreciation for cricket or its traditions and sought only to benefit himself and his crew, often at the expense and credibility of the game. He had been within a whisker of being given a significant ban for his involvement in match fixing and yet still lived very close to the line, playing inexplicable shots and displaying lamentable lapses in concentration in the field. Although highly suspicious in terms of match or spot fixing behaviour, none of it was enough to finger him. It remained the worst-kept secret in cricket that a chat with this gentleman would involve a circuitous and opaque reference to improving ones returns from the game if one could behave in a certain way at a specific time in a match.

It had been an interesting day, observing a criminal spending his money. Watching as he met a 'city gent' at The Trading House for coffee and a report on his portfolio. It seemed a curiously apt destination with its trophy animals hanging from the walls. He listened and observed from an adjacent table with amusement as the cricketer's eyebrows raised at his broker's suggestions, trying desperately to give the impression that he was completely across puts, calls and CDO's, while his man from the City continued the flood of arcane gibberish that passed for advice.

Coffee and confusion done with, it was a short walk to the Duck and Waffle for a late lunch with a group of four men who embodied the term 'wide boy' with such gusto and nonchalance it was as if they were in on the joke. Sadly, they weren't. They all wore the obligatory gold watches with faces the size of a pikelet and business shirts untucked in shades that were more Ted Baker than Thomas Pink. No self-respecting wide-boy outfit would be complete without an assortment of gold jewellery and sure enough, a combination of bangles, heavy neck chains and earrings glistened and flashed in the early afternoon sun. Their hair contained enough product to lubricate the 4th Fleet and their conversation was loud and ostentatious with the unmistakeable air of 'I may have been poor once but look at me now'.

The killer accepted a table within hearing distance and studied the menu with apparent interest as the conversation continued.

"Who's doing what, mate? I need to know where to put my money."

"Patience, my friend. Sometimes these things cannot be sorted until closer to the start of the match. I need to know who has been selected to play for a start."

"We're not just here to place your bets, we want some of the action."

A third man piped up. "And if anyone needs any extra encouragement to play ball, that can be arranged."

The cricketer winced inwardly. Although not a paragon of morality, he had no interest in seeing his fellow players hurt. He just wanted to make money.

"There will be no need for that. The guys I have are up for it and they know this is the only way players of their standard will become seriously rich from cricket."

"All right, but don't let us down." It was said with just enough menace to convey consequence and suddenly, the quirky combination of duck confit atop a toasted waffle lost some its joviality.

"Oi, love, more champagne over 'ere."

The conversation had moved on and the cricketer climbed into the vintage Taittinger in a manner not available to him in his place of birth.

When the lunch finally ended the group descended and dispersed across London. The killer followed his prey to an apartment in Knightsbridge and settled down to wait. If his normal patterns were observed, it would be an afternoon inside before heading out for dinner – all going well, his last.

47

"Have we found out where in the world I would find Pieter van Zyl?" Although trying to remain impassive, Dunn's tone betrayed the exasperation he was beginning to feel.

"Last spotted nursing a rum punch on Jumby Bay Island, sir. A bit of R'N'R in between T20 tournaments."

"So, we've got cricketers at risk in England, Antigua, New Zealand, Sri Lanka, India and wherever Faisal Shaikh happens to be at the moment. Marvellous." His sarcasm was largely in resignation as he realised that if the theory rang true, he had a very complex mix of cricketers and countries to patrol to say nothing of the risk of having a different opinion from that of the killer as to the make-up of the World XI.

"Get hold of all the guys we highlighted. Leave the South Africans as I've spoken to them and the Kirsten incident has them doubled down on security anyway. Most of them live in Escobarian seclusion but without suggesting they take bodyguards everywhere, tell them to take every reasonable precaution. If Trinnick has the various security agencies sorted, our killer is going to find it very hard to leave the country."

Wright spoke first. "Yes, interesting to think he has made it this far. India, Australia, Jamaica and now England. Gordy, how did you guys go on correlating travellers?"

"Well, Lu, Inspector Trinnick told me his team would look after that," answered Landolfi. "We were starting to draw some interesting conclusions and correlate some passports and arrivals but he said he would take it from there – seemed pretty adamant."

"I'll check in with him later. Now, our primary suspect was wearing a brand of suit made in New Zealand called Working Style. Now, with on-line shopping and people's propensity to travel that doesn't make it a certainty but let's work the New Zealand angle in our checks. I'll speak with the team combing through the travel details and get them to cut out all traveller's bar New Zealanders and Australians and cross-check all flights within two or three days either side of each murder. Those buggers like to travel but there can't be that many that have made that sequence of countries in recent months. You guys carry on with player locations and we'll check back in tomorrow. I'll go and see Trinnick and let him know where we're up to. And see if you can track down Faisal Shaikh – a man of his predilections is not likely to have nipped back to Islamabad once the Kolkata test was abandoned. My money is on him being in London. Check out where he normally stays – if such a place exists – and see if he's been at Lord's or The Oval for any of the county games. A perfect opportunity for the little snipe to drum up some business."

Dunn wandered down to Trinnick's office in the full expectation that the old curmudgeon would be behind his always cleared desk, tapping gently away on his keyboard or scanning the single file he had chosen to read. Dunn always winced when a return visit was made as he liked to keep everything he was working on within arm's reach. It was a near certainty that Trinnick would be there as his 8 am to 6 pm rituals while in the office were something of legend, only investigations and what his Outlook calendar always noted as 'Private Appointment' ever interfering with his routine.

Dunn knew there was nothing in the calendar for the afternoon, so was surprised to see an empty chair and a shutdown computer. Despite not having much concrete to report and part of him feeling relieved, he didn't have to impart his lack of progress. Dunn's nose told him something was up. Where the hell was he?

48

The killer watched as Faisal Shaikh left his apartment and wandered down Motcomb Street, heading for Salloos, a Knightsbridge restaurant specialising in Pakistani fare. It was his regular evening destination and he looked perfectly at home as he stopped across the road at the Nags Head for half a lager and a cigarette before he went into the restaurant. It wasn't long before a man joined him and relieved him of the backpack he had shouldered down the road. The killer smiled inwardly. Looks like something off to be laundered and I very much doubt it's gym gear.

It was just before seven o'clock when he was greeted at the entrance in a manner befitting a Test cricketer from Pakistan in a Pakistani restaurant. He followed the owner through the restaurant and took a seat at a quiet table toward the back, ignoring the hopeful eyes desperate for acknowledgment. Not surprisingly, it was only women whose eyes were met and held just long enough to provide a momentary air of tension at their tables. Shaikh was not the best-looking man to have played for Pakistan but was living proof of the power of status.

The owner had a bottle of Dom Perignon waiting and poured two flutes without delay.

"Good evening, Faisal, how was your day today? You must be hungry but let's enjoy a drink first."

"Well, I had quite a good lunch but there is always room for some of your fine fare. Tell me, is the young lady who served us on Wednesday here tonight?"

"Unfortunately, not, but let's not have that worry us. We will be well looked after."

The owner tried to give off the air of 'friendly uncle' and enjoyed the halo that Faisal brought his restaurant, but he had decided against playing quasi-pimp for a rat bag like this.

At the front of the restaurant, the killer took his seat. He was amused to see Isabel Sauvignon Blanc on the wine list. Although he didn't drink a lot of 'savvy', he ordered a glass as homage to his home country. It was the perfect spot to observe, then to track and then to kill.

Faisal tucked into his Shahi Kofta and a couple of kebabs. His appetite had recovered from his lunchtime indigestion and an afternoon nap had him perked up, enjoying his Dom and looking forward to his Bhuna Gosht.

"Tell me, Faisal," the owner asked. "Where shall I put my money? You have some connections in the money world and I have a sum I'd like to see grow faster than what a deposit in the NatWest is likely to do."

"Ha, don't ask me, I'm just a cricketer." He reflected on the advice he received that morning. Would it really hurt to give this man a steer? No, it was his opportunity. He'd taken all the risk and he was paying the fees to get the tips. This man was getting his celebrity – that was quite enough.

The dinner meandered through a range of conversations, none of particular interest to Faisal and after the second bottle of champagne was nearly exhausted,he felt that it was time to head for home. Tomorrow would require all his persuasion to add some new faces to his fixing set.

As he rose, a man approached the table at a speed just below threatening.

"Faisal, remember me?"

Shaikh feigned indifference but it was certainly a face he remembered.

"Yes, Mr Dunn, I do recall you. You tried to convict me without evidence and all hell broke loose."

Dunn was tempted to bite but let it go. Shaikh gathered his phone and man-bag and began to rise.

"Faisal, sit down for a minute, will you? We need to talk."

"Do we, Mr Dunn? I'm not sure I'm interested in anything you have to say. If you'll excuse me, I was just heading home."

"Believe me, you'll want to hear this. Please, just sit down. We won't be long."

"OK." He gestured to the owner. "Thank you for dinner. Could you give us some privacy, please?" The owner departed with the hint of a deferential nod and Shaikh eyed Dunn with a practiced indifference.

"Right, Mr Dunn, what can I do for you?"

"Well, despite our differences in the past, it's actually about me doing something for you. You're no doubt aware of the murders of some the world's best cricketers over the past month."

"Yes, I am. None of them friends of mine but I respected them as cricketers." He didn't add that he'd had 500 quid on Andy Beaumont to meet his demise – it seemed you really could get a bet on anything if you knew the right people. "So, what does this have to do with me?"

"Well, Faisal, we have a theory that this person might be murdering a group of players as a means of 'selecting' a World XI. We don't know why but going by the rankings and some of your recent performances, it is likely that you are a candidate."

"Interesting, Mr Dunn. I suppose that is right. I am worthy of a place in that team. Who else would open the batting?"

"That's just it. You're on obvious selection, particularly as our other theory is that this could all be something of a moral crusade, with your reputation, you're a candidate on both fronts."

The air quietly left the table and the faux cordiality disappeared.

"Mr Dunn, you keep on about something for which I was never convicted. Thank you for the warning but I live 500 metres down the road – and it's likely I will have company. I'd like to leave now."

"No problem but you've been warned. Take care, Faisal, and not just tonight. If you see or hear someone that looks threatening or even a bit dodgy, let me know."

The silence that followed suggested the conversation was over and Dunn turned and moved briskly past the tables toward the restaurant's entrance. Oddly, half a glass of white wine sat on one of the tables with no diner in sight, and no one had passed his conversation with Shaikh to go to the bathroom. He motioned to the waiter.

"Did the person who started this glass of wine have a reservation?"

"No, sir, he was a walk-in. He ordered a glass of wine, put ten pounds on the table and left. I didn't even see him go."

Curious behaviour, he thought, but something was nagging him as he pushed through the door and headed for home.

49

Faisal Shaikh was just inebriated enough to remain carefree about Dunn's warning. The thought that someone would kill him between now and the security of his apartment in Knightsbridge was absurd.

The killer watched from the pub across the road. He had expected the complication of a young woman accompanying him, as this had been his habit recently. Tonight, he was alone, too many champagnes to maintain a steady gait and likely to be clumsy and defenceless in the face of attack. Perfect.

Only a few blocks distant, Dunn was enjoying the walk home, smiling at the ostentation of the Lamborghinis and the young boys filming every rev from their super-charged engines. As he passed Harrods, he paused. *Was that really good enough? Oh, Faisal, there's a mad man out there, take care old son – toodle pip*! The half-empty wine glass returned to the forefront of his mind. Someone had scarpered soon after he'd walked in. Could be nothing but getting to Shaikh is the only way I'm going to confirm that. The carelessness that had been a factor in the Da Silva disaster was not going to be repeated now. Fortunately, Landolfi had provided an address for where Shaikh lived while in London, so he moved quickly back in the direction from whence he'd come. It was his best chance to protect someone directly. Lord knows what he would do with the international candidates.

He took a short-cut and darted through Hans Crescent, past the Ecuadorean embassy and on to Sloane St. His destination was just a few hundred metres away and he hoped he would have a chance to catch Faisal before he settled in for the night. Theirs was not a relationship that suggested a cosy chat over a Scotch.

As he approached Shaikh's flat, he saw him leaning on the wrought-iron fence that fronted his apartment. His arms were either side of his head and Dunn smirked at the thought of Shaikh emptying his perfectly cooked curry all over the basement flat. Too many bubblies Faisal, old boy.

"Faisal, how are you? Bit worse for wear? Rather spoils the theory you can't get crook on the good stuff, eh?" Shaikh offered nothing back.

"Jeepers, you are gone. You seemed fine at dinner, are you?"

Dunn touched Shaikh and hoped he would look up through a post-vomit glaze but it was not to be. His body seemed to swivel on his head, which was either remarkable balance for a man a couple to the wind or as was in fact the case, his face had been staved through one of the spikes on the fence.

Dunn leant next to him, head lowered.

"Fuck."

50

After a morning interviewing Garth Kirsten (which had done little to advance the case apart to confirm that a well-built man was the perpetrator) and checking in with Landolfi and Wright about leads from Shaikh's demise (there were none), Mike Dunn made his way up the A10 bound for Cambridge, excited at the prospect of finally reacquainting with Alpa. He felt a bit silly about having agreed to meet in the town centre but it wasn't polite expecting Alpa to find a pub in a small village in the middle of the county. It would also afford a bit time to chat during the twenty-minute drive down to the Chequers in Fowlmere.

As he approached the pick-up point, Dunn was delighted to see Alpa already there and even more delighted at the cheerful wave and pretty smile she unleashed as he drew to a stop on the corner. Alpa jumped in and accepted a quick kiss to the cheek before strapping in as Dunn accelerated into the steady late-morning traffic.

Although trying earnestly to remain focused on the road, Mike found Alpa's appearance quite breath taking. A short summer dress with a Liberty print complemented her navy flats and the fresh scent of her perfume completed what he considered quite a stunning package. Her tone was gentle and her conversation fluid but she was content to let Dunn's music fill the gaps, despite the odd giggle at some of the more doubtful material on his Spotify playlist.

"Hey, what's wrong with a bit of Duran?" he responded in mock defence.

"Hmm, nothing if you're an 18-year-old girl in 1986, Mike."

He skipped to the next song, hoping it might restore some cred but only Kajagoogoo's *Too Shy* made it through the speakers.

Alpa clapped and squealed, "Wow, great tunes, Mike. Don't suppose you have anything from this century?"

Dunn grinned and accelerated down the M11, keen to have a drink and enjoy the late summer warmth. Although brief, an afternoon away from the rampage of the serial killer would be just the salve for his increasingly jaded mind.

They found a seat in the beer garden and Dunn walked in to buy their drinks, a rose from Provence for her and a lager from The Netherlands for him. They got through some ice-breaker material and conversation was coming easily but Dunn couldn't help but ask about Faisal Shaikh.

"Sorry to throw a bit of business in but what did you make of the conversation you overheard back in Kolkata?"

"It was weird. The players seemed to be there to relax and have a few drinks and Shaikh was like a crown prosecutor crossed with an insurance salesman – question after question, just boxing them into a corner. Some of the groups splintered off but those that remained seemed really interested in what he had to say. Unfortunately, my good-looking friend brought the conversation to an end, so all I heard was a few ideas and suggestions but it wasn't hard to interpret the intent."

"Yes, we'd felt he'd been involved in this for some time but could never piece enough evidence together to catch him. The one time we got close, I stuffed up big time. But we won't be getting anything out of him now. Anyway, enough of that. What are your plans now? Where do you see yourself living?"

"I'm not really sure, Mike. I'd love to stay here but my parents are in India and, of course, there are a huge amount of opportunities in New York for my particular field."

Settling into a second pint and another glass of rose they chatted about events since their flight together and their thwarted 'first date'. Alpa had spent a few weeks in Kolkata before returning for the start of the new term and had seen much of the coverage concerning the murdered cricketers.

"Mike, do you think you're in danger? The killer obviously knows it is you who is trying to catch him."

"Possibly but at the moment he is outpacing me at every turn. The closest I've got is being in the same hotel but he might as well have been on the other side of the Thames."

"What is his end game? I mean, how many cricketers is he going to kill?"

"We really don't know, although, and strictly confidentially, we believe he might be trying pick some form of super team. But enough of that. Tell me about your prospects in New York."

"Hmm, not sure if there is much to tell. My doctorate is on corporate finance and social responsibility and it's attracting some attention. A couple of the big banks have expressed interest, but that's all it is for now."

She looked at Mike with eyes too soft to be called a stare but still unerringly direct. "Besides, I'm not sure where I want to live. And I'd like to think being in England has some possibilities."

Mike Dunn could barely suppress a grin and eased out of the moment by suggesting he grab some menus from inside.

He strolled back in from the beer garden, feeling incredibly buoyed for the first time since well before Mistry was killed. With glasses replenished, he paused at the window and looked at Alpa's profile and the comfort with which she accepted second glances from the Sunday afternoon crowd. As he returned to the table, his phone lit up and began to buzz across the surface. Seeing 'Jolian Ford-Robertson' come up on the top of his phone was not an immediate downer as he was hoping for some forensic news on the cricket stump which was used so severely on Garth Kirsten.

"Sorry, Alpa, I'd better take this. Won't be a minute."

"Jolian, what's up?" he answered as he walked over to an unoccupied table. "Got some good news for me, I hope?"

"Wish I had, Mike, but you're not going to like this. Trinnick has called a press conference for 4 pm this afternoon. You're expected to be here."

Dunn was distraught and utterly baffled in the same moment. Quite what they had to share with press was a mystery and why call it for Sunday afternoon? What was Trinnick playing at? He approached the table gingerly.

"Alpa, I'm terribly sorry, but I've been called back to London."

"What is it, Mike? Has there been another murder?"

"No, nothing like that, thank God. My boss has called a press conference, which is just completely strange, but I've got to be there. I'm sorry but I'm going to have to get going. Let's get you an Uber. I'm so sorry about this."

"Mike, it's fine. It wasn't how I saw the afternoon ending either, so let's try again, maybe when this case is behind you."

Dunn took the inference despite the gentle delivery. *Trinnick, you bastard,* he thought as he ushered her through the pub. *You utter fucking bastard.*

With Alpa headed back to Cambridge, he turned on to the A10 for the trip back to London. A few minutes into the trip, the phone started to ring with Trinnick's name displayed at the top of the device.

"Mike, how are you? I presume you've heard the news. I'm getting the press together this afternoon and need an hour or so with you prior just to get the message clear and the facts aligned."

Dunn was furious. He clearly wasn't going to be needed at the press conference and yet here he was, heading back to London to do something that could easily have been achieved by phone.

"OK, sir, I'm on my way. See you at the office?"

"Yes, that would be good. Shouldn't be long and you can get back to whatever it is you do with your weekends. Oh, and if you could bring your laptop, that would be appreciated. I want to put some slides up."

Dunn sensed the terseness and wondered what had caused this abrupt change in behaviour from Trinnick. He had always been serious and manic about detail but his upbringing insisted that manners and civility were paramount, even when – or particularly when – one was under pressure. This change of tone and unusually random act of calling a press conference was puzzling.

"OK, I'll need to nip home and grab it, so I'll probably park at home and grab a train to the office. Should be there by threeish."

"Thank you, Mike, see you then." The click arrived well before a response could be made.

51

He sensed the blow before he felt it. As he turned the key to make it into his apartment, he heard the swish of an object narrowing in on the back of his neck. In the microseconds prior to contact, Dunn had just enough time to think *I'm in a bit of trouble here,* but not enough time to take meaningful evasive action. The blow was significant, landing with enough force to propel Dunn forward onto the front door of his apartment. As he pivoted to confront his attacker, the second blow hit him on the side of the knee, only his fingers clinging to the architraves stopping him from being prostrate and completely at his attacker's mercy. As it happened, prostrate might have been a better bet as blow three hammered into the back of his kidneys and blow four took care of said clinging fingers.

"Stay the fuck out of the way, Dunn. You can't stop me and if I feel like you are going to get in the way. You've seen how easy it is for me to finish you. I have no quarrel with you but that can soon change."

Had he not been a little stunned, he might have thought twice about responding with 'Fuck off' but it was out before sense could play a role. The next blow to the back of the head ended the discussion and with it, any chance Dunn would avoid hospital treatment.

"Mild concussion, badly bruised ribs, head laceration and two broken fingers." Dunn could hear the rather mellifluous tones of a young woman reading out a menu of injuries and it took a moment or two for him to realise this was his 'run chart'. Certainly all the listed pieces hurt like hell and as he woke properly, he recognised Lucinda Wright standing in his ward chatting to the nurse.

"He's bloody lucky, you know. He's been hit with what must have been a truncheon or an iron bar, so his injuries could have been far more severe. In fact, the only good news is that whoever did this didn't want him dead. He clearly could have finished him off, no bother."

168

"Thank you, nurse. Can you give us a moment? I'd like to speak to him as soon as he wakes up."

The nurse considered this request but the look in Wright's eyes suggested 'Yes' would be a good response. "Sure, I've got to see a few more patients and then I'll nip back and top up his meds. Have me paged before you leave, though."

"No problem." Wright closed the door and turned to see Dunn smiling at her.

"Hi, Lu, jolly good of you to pop in. I think our man has taken offence to our investigation. It might mean we're getting close."

"Are you sure it was him? It could have just been a random attack, couldn't it?"

"No, it was him all right. Gave me a pretty unambiguous message after the first few blows. Told us to back off so I told him to Fuck Off."

"Yes, I can see why that might have stifled the pleasantries. Did you get a look at him?"

"No chance. He dealt to me pretty well and I suspect he knocked me out with one of the blows. Can't even tell you if he was big, small, strong or weak. Mind you, you don't have to be Jason Statham to take someone out from behind with an iron bar."

"I know you've just been given a bit of a beating, Mike, but Gordon and I need to keep moving on Faisal Shaikh's murder. I've asked Trinnick to alert customs and Gordon is with the staff at the Pakistani restaurant right now. Anything else we should be doing?"

"I need you to call the other players on our list and then start thinking about security for them. It's time to put a ring around these guys and at least make this bastard work."

"Will do, Mike. I'll pop in tomorrow and give you an update."

"I'm not sure I'm going to be here. I need to speak to Garth Kirsten again and then I'm going to take a couple of days off. After that, I'm going back to India. Misra's an old friend and I'll be buggered if I'm going to let this psychopath get close to him. I'll be available by phone, so we can keep connected on the broader investigation but I want to see to Abhi Misra's security myself."

She leant forward and put her hands on the railing which surrounded the bed. "Mike, the nurse has expressly asked me to wait until she has spoken to you and topped up your medication. I know you like to think of yourself as a bit of a hard nut but given the injuries you've got are largely internal, you'd be taking a huge risk."

Dunn knew that Wright was spot on but he couldn't leave Misra as prey. "No worse than a decent towelling from the Leicester forward pack in the old days. Now, if you could grab that nurse, I'll dose up and be on my way. Oh, by the way, how did the press conference go?"

Wright's forehead creased just slightly. "Press conference?"

52

Although loathe to be seen as fleeing, Abhishek Misra had taken Dunn's advice and headed for Goa. The spate of murders that followed Mistry's demise had increased his unease with every tweet and although Goa was hardly out of reach for a resourceful murderer, he felt there would be ample security to keep him and his family safe. He'd contemplated any number of countries but all provided reasons not to bother. Iceland – he'd be a touch conspicuous. Fiji – about due for another coup or Pakistan – probably better off going toe to toe with the murderer. Although not given to conceit, if this guy was building a World XI as Dunn had texted, there was a fair chance he'd get the nod, so he'd taken his family for a few weeks of relaxation and a chance for the sort of precious together time that had become increasingly uncommon for international cricketers.

He stretched on his lounger under Goa's early sunshine. A workout, a swim and some time with the morning papers at the beach was a fine way to start the day after all the trauma of recent weeks. He suppressed a grin as the latest text from his daughter lit up his screen. She had taken to sending messages from her mother's phone and her creative use of emojis was part of an ongoing cryptic joust between the two of them, each sending messages that were self-evident to their writer but often utterly confusing for the recipient. How he was supposed to know that two trophies, a hen and a knife and fork became 'winner, winner, chicken dinner'? Misra had achieved a first at Oxford and had hoped for a more classical range from his daughter but popular culture and early exposure to social media had soon put paid to that.

Up until recently, life had worked as planned for Misra. By now, a certain selection in the national team and a regular in the IPL, he enjoyed a stable family life with his wife and daughter and a phenomenal income to a level where the Imperator suite at the Grand Hyatt in Goa was a given rather than an excess. The murders had made Misra question everything – would immediate retirement take him out of the sights of the murderer? Was he even in danger? Why hadn't this guy been caught? Pradip Mistry was not a great friend but he was a colleague and the thought of him and the other greats being 'dismissed' in this way was terrifying.

He'd just made it to the sports section of the *The New York Times* when his phone rang.

"Hi, Mike. How are you?"

"Good, Abhi, and you?"

"I'm well. I thought a lot about what you said and, in the end, agreed that your suggestion had merit, so I'm speaking to you from Goa."

"Good to hear, Abhi, but listen, we don't know where the killer is. I'm pretty sure he has just killed Faisal Shaikh. It's unimaginable that you would not be on his list."

"When you say, you think he has killed Shaikh, are you saying that he has been killed?"

"I'm afraid so. I know he wasn't either of our idea of friendship material but we have lost another of the game's best. The World XI theory is getting even more realistic, which is really why I've called. Heighten whatever security measures you have taken. Where are you staying?"

"I'm at the Hyatt. They deal with this celebrity stuff all the time." He paused in embarrassment at his self-inclusion. "Sorry, they manage celebrity security all the time – not that I include myself in that bracket but if I have a word, I'm sure they'll be equipped to deal with it."

"OK, Abhi, but take care. Look, I've decided to head out and be a part of the security arrangements. He might just push his luck and give us the chance to apprehend him. Stay vigilant in the meantime though, Abhi, this guy is like a ghost."

"I will, Mike. Thanks for calling."

Misra had finished the last of his papers and thought it's time for a quick drink and then back up to see his family for breakfast. He signalled to the waiter and requested a mineral water with a slice of lemon, then settled back to enjoy the view and bask for a few moments longer. A few moments became a few minutes, which puzzled him. The service in Goa is legendary and Misra, although a humble man, was on the edge of irritation at the delay in his drink's arrival. Glancing toward the bar, he was amazed to see no one there and certainly no one attending to what he thought was a reasonable and reasonably basic request. He was on the verge of heading back to the suite when a waiter appeared, offering apologies and laying out the napkin and drink as if it were a flute of Pol Roger rather than a humble ice water.

The morning had warmed and Misra gulped greedily at the promise of refreshment. *What is wrong with the lemon?* he thought as the water hit his taste buds. *Either that or they haven't opened a fresh bottle* as the usual sensation at the back of his throat didn't eventuate. The lemon was in fact picked from a tree that morning and couldn't have been fresher – the water was from a newly opened San Pellegrino. The sallow flavour was predominantly down to the killer's poison and as Misra's throat tightened in tune with his body's convulsions, the formation of the World XI became one player closer.

53

Dunn rolled over in bed. Although he'd prepared for his first night back at home with some Endones and splash or two of Glenmorangie, their respective tranquillising effects were long exhausted by the time he'd woken. The kidney damage meant a particularly uncomfortable pit stop first thing and his taped-up fingers meant everything happened at geriatric speed. The bruising on the knee and the stitches in the back of his head he could deal with but the small things were exasperating. Balancing his toothbrush on the vanity, coating it carefully with one hand, reaching for it to clean his teeth and watching it tip on its side produced an unseemly rant, only exceeded by the tirade which followed his unsuccessful efforts to remove a screw cap from a bottle of Tamar Ridge Pinot Noir while clamping it with his underarm.

Everyday tasks aside, the attack had unsettled Dunn. His work in crime had always involved him in pursuit of the 'bad guys'. When the chase was over, the hands went up, the cuffs were applied (metaphorically if not physically) generally with little more than a scuffle but more often than not with a resigned look and an acknowledgment of futility. Now, Dunn had gone from somewhere near the top of the food chain to just another one of its constituent parts – a killer blow to the bravado and self-assurance. It wasn't so much the pain and the damaged parts but more the psychological shift from being the hunter to the victim. Would he return? Would he select other methods of harm? Does he know about Gordon and Lucinda – probably, no, obviously – and what about families? Then again, where do they fit in terms of motive? He was building a World XI, so why would he risk capture chasing investigators? Hoping it was a one-off and that he would be the only target was like working through the odds of being taken by a shark – a solid bet against until you see the fin.

The recent weeks of travel and investigation had left Dunn's provisions on the light side, both in terms of food and life essentials. Although a firm believer in not over-burdening your fridge when there are myriad options within walking distance, he did accept that Lucinda Wright's expression of horror was probably justified when she opened the fridge, having kindly brought over a couple of meals to help him through his convalescence. It was a toss-up whether expiry dates or the lack of vegetables was her primary source of discomfort but it was clear she felt that Dunn hadn't quite made the transition from student flat to moderately wealthy bachelor. As she had promised to return with a top-up, he decided a trip to the local supermarket was in order. Although not overly concerned with Lucinda's view of his domestic operation, there was a certain pride in a base level of competence. Besides, he was down to his last bottle of Pinot and had run out of tonic.

Given his injuries and his general loathing of the concept, he was pleased a mini version of a supermarket was just around the corner and that he would be shopped and back on his couch in no time. On checking for opening hours, he was curious to see that no fewer than 165 people had written reviews of the place. While not a participant in social media – and therefore accepting of the fact that its charms and usefulness may have escaped him – he did feel that 165 people giving their view of the Little Waitrose in Knightsbridge was probably not what Berners-Lee had in mind when he started the project.

He had done the milk, eggs and bread and thrown in a couple of packets of eye fillet when his phone rang. Jolian Ford-Robertson's name came up on the screen.

He took a couple of steps into a quiet part of the produce section but it soon became clear from Jolian's tone this was not about fingerprints or trace elements.

"Mike, bad news. Abhishek Misra is dead. You need to get to Goa."

"Oh, Jesus, no, not Abhi, I only spoke to him a day or so back. Look, I'm booked on a plane to Goa later this week but there's bugger all point now. I'm out of the house now but I need you to get Gordon and Lu over to mine as soon as you can."

Abandoning his groceries, he made his way back to his apartment as quickly as his dodgy leg would allow. "How the hell did he get to Abhi? How the hell did he get through immigration? There is just no way this guy is doing this without help – what the hell was Trinnick doing?"

Rattling keys let Dunn know that his colleagues had arrived. He was utterly relieved that Lu had his spare set as getting up and down from the couch was the perfect way to reacquaint himself with every blow the killer had inflicted on him.

Landolfi put a tray of coffees down as Wright grabbed a plate and arranged some pastries on it. Landolfi hadn't seen Dunn since the mugging and tried to conceal his shock.

"Morning, Mike. Crap couple of days, how're you holding up?"

"I've been better, Gordy, but for now, my physical well-being is quite a way down the list. Let's get a plan together. Where do we think he is going to strike next and when?"

"I've actually made a bit of progress on who as well. This Marty Fowler is an interesting individual, Mike. Star cricketer as a youngster and went to the World Youth tournament. Looks like he was involved in some form of off-field incident as he was sent home for disciplinary reasons just before the business end of the tournament. Sadly for him, he had a nasty accident in his last year at school and doesn't appear to have played again. Made a pile of money in a very short space of time and in the last few years seems to have slipped off the radar. Not quite off the grid but certainly nothing to get him up the list on a Google search."

"OK, good work, Gordy. Any idea on where he is now?"

"He left New Zealand about five weeks ago. Boarded a plane to Singapore and then got a connecting flight to Mumbai. We're working on next steps but if you're wondering, he could definitely have got to Kolkata by the time of Mistry's murder."

"Bloody hell. Motive escapes me but if the reports on his wealth are accurate, then 'means' is well taken care of. If he's our killer – and he's as good a candidate as we've got right now, we need to double down on the background. Gordy, see if you can get some photos of him. There must be something from his playing days and if he made a pile of money in New Zealand at a young age, there are bound to be profiles of him somewhere. I'm sure the tall poppy brigade would have had a crack at him too. We've got to find something else can we connect him to and if anything might have happened at that tournament to motivate his spree? The one thing we've agreed on from the start is that these killings are personal – so if he's our man, what the hell went down at that cricket tournament?"

Lu leaned forward. "No argument on the investigation of Fowler but what about right now? This guy has a team to complete and he's not giving me a 'that'll be all for the moment' feeling."

"Spot on, Lu. I need one of you to get to Goa and see if there is anything we can get from the crime scene. With Gordon trying to piece together Fowler's life and current movements, that looks like it's going to be you. OK with that?"

"Marvellous," she replied in a manner which nearly disguised the sarcasm. "I'd always imagined my first trip to Goa would involve endless massages and intravenous cocktails but at least I get out of going to Gino's parents this weekend – if I don't eat my body-weight in pasta, I'm somehow unappreciative."

"I might let that one go through to the keeper, Lu. Get yourself on a flight as soon as you can and keep me abreast of anything the crime scene elicits. I've got to get ahead of this guy and it looks to me that the Sri Lankan spinner, Wickramysinghe might be the logical next step in terms of geography. The murderer will end up in New Zealand eventually, as he must have his sights on Cam Peters but for the moment, I need a ticket to Galle."

54

Lucinda Wright landed at Dabolim Airport after a short stop in Doha. She was relieved to see that a member of the investigative team had been assigned to collect her and she dozed during the short trip through Vasco De Gama and down to the Hyatt resort by Arossim beach. As she put her suitcase on the luggage tray and unpacked a change of clothes and some toiletries, she couldn't help but feel this was a low-value assignment, given the killer's hit-and-split modus operandi. The only place he'd spent much time was England but his alleged appearance had given him the opportunity to blend in, much better than he would in Kolkata, Kingston or indeed Goa.

Although in doubt about the value of this part of the investigation, this was beginning to look like a career-defining case. Stopping the killer and making an arrest would no doubt lead to promotion and a surging reputation. The corollary would mean those who had quashed her aspirations previously would feel vindicated. Wright had been the 'person to watch' in the early part of her career, revolutionising the way the organisation worked and transforming it from a ponderous boy's club to an effective, inclusive crime solving force. It was as if Lara Croft had marched into the St James Club and asked if there were any objections to her becoming a member. Leadership of the division was viewed as a when, not if, proposition until the cocky Londoner who had no idea how she had improved the organisation came in and told everyone how he could make it better. She spent a year quietly fuming but despite herself, couldn't help but admit he was good to have around and if pressed, would acknowledge that she actually enjoyed his company. Now, both she and Mike Dunn needed this case very badly.

Returning to the lobby, she was greeted by a distinguished-looking gentleman, clad in a pale blue suit, white shirt and black loafers. A neatly trimmed beard and carefully combed hair suggested businessman rather than policeman but he announced himself as the latter as he approached with arm outstretched.

"Ms Wright, I'm Subro Singhal. I'm in charge of the local investigative team."

"Hello, Mr Singhal. Shall we."

"Please, call me Subro," he interrupted. "How would you like to progress things?"

"Well, let's start at the start. Do we know if our killer stayed here or did he find a way past security?"

"We think he was a house guest but can't be sure about this as a number of guests checked out in the hour or so either side of Misra's murder. The nature of his death meant no one knew he was dead for some time after. It was assumed he was relaxing on the lounger and the staff are trained to be unobtrusive."

"Good grief, I've seen the pictures of the body. That's hardly a guy assuming a normal pose on a lounger. I don't mean to be indelicate but he looks like a dead insect."

"I agree, Ms Wright, but either way, assessment of staff protocol will not help with this investigation."

"The other curious bit for me is how we have Abhi Misra ordering an iced-water with a slice of lemon and between the barman making it and delivering it, someone slipped in sufficient poison to render him dead within seconds of it passing his lips."

"I believe, Ms Wright," said Singhal, raising an index finger for emphasis, "that the division of labour is rather strict. A barman would make the drink and a waiter would then deliver it. Standard procedure in a hotel of this nature."

"Yes, I get that, but how does our killer get the poison in without anyone noticing?"

"Well, Ms Wright, I am pleased to say that is something I can help with. If you wouldn't mind coming this way, I can show you the security footage. I think it will clarify the killer's method."

They made their way through the lobby and took the lift to the first floor. Singhal gestured for her to enter one of the small conference rooms, which she saw contained numerous screens, a couple of technicians and a line-up of manila folders on the side table against the far wall. Wright felt both impressed by the professionalism and mildly embarrassed about her preconceived notion of what the investigation might look like.

"As you know, my remit is to solve this crime and this crime only. I understand it fits into a bigger picture but as I say, my first job is to determine how and by whom this particular crime has taken place. I have assembled a specialist team to work through any technological clues and I think you will be impressed with what they have come up with. Please, have a seat in front of this monitor."

As she sat down, an impish young man appeared at her shoulder. He wore a plain white short-sleeved shirt and black trousers with shiny shoes straight out of the schoolyard. Everything about him from the neck down appeared to be regulation kit. Heading north, a spider-web tattoo connected his shoulders to the array of studs in his left ear, which was partially obscured by a shock of black hair. The right side of his head was shaved to the scalp, revealing 'MCMCX', which could have meant anything from his birth year to Sachin Tendulkar's test debut. She didn't ask.

"This is Vineet, our IT and communications expert. He used to be a troublesome hacker but we have decided that he is better working with us than languishing in gaol. Vineet has been responsible for working through the various pieces of footage from the security cameras. You asked how the poison was administered – have a look at this."

Singhal gestured to Vineet and he clicked on the arrow in the middle of the screen to start the clip. Wright watched as the barman worked through the relatively simple process of compiling an ice water, uncapping the San Pellegrino and slicing the lemon with some brisk strokes of what appeared to be a samurai knife. He placed the drink on a tray and put the tray up on the service area ready for collection and delivery.

"OK, slow this bit, Vinny. Watching, watching…now hit pause and run it in slow motion."

Wright was stunned. A white-jacketed hand reached across as if ready to collect the tray and make the delivery but instead, his palm opened and a sprinkle of white powder resembling the contents of a Stevia was shown falling on to the surface of the drink.

"Nice work, Vineet," said Wright, clapping enthusiastically. "I guess we've got the method sorted but that doesn't help me identify who owns the hand. Throughout the investigation, we've been looking for a well-built man with something of a limp. Have you any footage from around the hotel in the last few days that might help us confirm our prime suspect was here?"

Vineet grinned and his head gave an almost imperceptible wobble of delight. "I'm glad you asked that, Ms Wright. Yes, I have been scouring the footage from every camera in the hotel. Of course, the only place a guest is guaranteed to be filmed is the check-in desk, so I have focussed my effort on this camera. Have a look at this, shot just after lunch two days ago."

A broad-shouldered man stood in line, apparently waiting patiently to check-in. As the clerk smiled and gestured him forward, his gait broke and he limped toward the counter.

"OK, that's him – it's got to be! Tell me you've got the name he checked in under?" Wright sat back and waited as Vineet scrolled through the guest list.

"Vineet, I'm looking for a Martin Fowler. Can you see his name?"

"I won't be able to give you the exact person but I can give you the names of all those who checked in around the time we can see your suspect. Clearly, women and those of Indian origin can be excluded, so we will have a very short list. OK, hmmm, it won't be Habeeb Khaja, it's not Emma Sarafian." As he searched, he tapped a pen against his teeth, which was as soothing as a Bjork album track. "I'm sorry. The most likely match is this guy – Ian Michael Heamana. Not the name you were looking for, I'm afraid."

"No, it's not but the timing is right, so let's stay with him. Can you find out what room he was in? Text me when you have it. I'm heading for the lobby. Thanks for your help you guys, great work."

Within seconds of entering the lobby, her phone beeped and a text with a room number appeared. She leant on the reception desk and beckoned the duty manager closer.

"Hi there, I need access to this room," she said, offering up her phone. "I'm part of the crew investigating Mr Misra's death."

"Certainly, madam," came the response. "If I could just see some identification, I can give you immediate access."

Wright bristled but fished out her ID. "There you are."

The manager returned the ID and a small wallet with a plastic room key within.

Wright entered the room, feeling just slightly apprehensive about what she might find, including the rooms most recent guest. She scanned the fixtures, looking for anything that might have suggested a rapid departure but found only order. The shape of the pillows suggested the occupant had slept alone. A chair placed perfectly under the desk and a lone towel lying on the floor of the bathroom suggested normal usage by a business traveller or a single occupant. The mini bar remained intact apart from an emptied bottle of Scotch and the iron remained on the surface atop the fridge. It was only when she opened the wardrobe door that her heart rate went up. Hanging there was a waiter's uniform, still looking pressed and pristine but Wright felt certain that examination would reveal it had indeed been used – just enough to slide through the service area, poison Misra's drink and head back to the room, just another staff member moving unobtrusively through the hotel.

She grabbed her mobile. "Subro, please, get you forensic team up here. Nothing certain but I'm pretty sure our killer was the occupant. Let's see what he left behind. In the meantime, I'm going to check back in with London. I'll call you in an hour or so. On second thoughts, let's meet in the bar. I'll see you about 4."

Gordon Landolfi answered on the second ring. "Hi, Lu, how are things in majestic Goa? Getting some sun on that winter complexion?"

"That'll do, Gordy. I'm certain our man was here. We've got CCTV of him in the lobby and he's the quintessential tall guy with a limp. Clearly, he's not so fond of using his real name, so I was hoping you could run a check on an Ian Michael Heamana. He used a New Zealand driver's licence as photo ID when he checked in but that's all we have apart from the fact that he had a waiter's uniform in the room he stayed in. He's our guy and if that's his real name, then I'm Sofia Vergara's body double."

"Well, I'm picking you think that's unlikely."

"Nailed it, Gordy – can you run it while I'm on the line?"

"Will do, Lu. Let's see if we can find out more about Mr Heamana."

Landolfi began hammering on the keys like a back-street masseuse and, not for the first time, Lucinda feared for the safety of the keyboard.

"Let's see, it certainly gives him a New Zealand flavour."

"Heamana's a Maori name?"

"That's its origin, yes." Landolfi breathed heavily down the line. "Oh, you're joking."

"What is it, Gordy?"

"It seems our assassin has a sense of humour. I've just picked up the English translation of *heamana*."

"Really? What is it?"

"The name Heamana means 'Chairman' in Maori."

"I'm waiting for the punchline here."

"Don't you see? He's selecting a cricket team and he's used the initials I and M for his first two names. Put them together and add his surname."

"Oh, that smart bastard. I.M. Chairman. I'm 'chairman of selectors'."

55

Cam Peters was a rarity among cricket's elite. For a start, he came from New Zealand – a land where great rugby players seem to grow on trees but great cricketers arrive once in a decade or two. The fact that two of their greatest players were in the same team explains much of the success of the Kiwis in the '80s and early '90s. Martin Crowe and Richard Hadlee were acknowledged the world over as masters of their craft and it was a long time before a new name was drawn in the same breath. Many players had great moments – Greatbatch's unbeaten hundred in Perth and Astle's double hundred in Christchurch but no one could claim parity with Crowe or Hadlee until one player emerged who was better than both. Cam Peters was the player the tiny nation had dreamt about.

Peters was different from the world's elite for another reason. Laid back compared to the intensity of his peers, open and friendly compared to their reticence and with a view on training that was diametrically opposed to the obsessives, who vied with him for the number-one ranking in world cricket. Although smart enough to realise that without being superbly fit his gifts would not be given full expression, weight programmes and beep tests did nothing for him. Fitness could be achieved in many ways and for Peters, there was no substitute for long hours at the bowling crease and even longer hours in the surf.

For the long hours at the bowling crease, there was no better place than with his mates at the Greerton Cricket Club. A good session in the nets, where his teammates would try and flog him to all parts was a regular staple in his pre-season training. 'The boys' would bat like men possessed to ensure Cam not only went wicketless but also had to do a fair bit of fetching once he had ball in hand. When they pushed things to far, they were reminded just why Cam was considered one of the game's foremost all-rounders. After training, it was down to Astrolabe on Mt Maunganui's main drag, where there was always a cold Heineken or two in readiness.

It was rare that Cam Peters missed a cricket training but it was inconceivable that he would miss a surf.

Surfing is a sport that doesn't know about time. There is no half-time, no bad light and certainly no stoppages for rain. Quite simply, if the surf is right, the time is right. Mt Maunganui does not have prodigious surf but the waves are regular enough and large enough to attract legions of surfers to the Bay of Plenty. Cam Peters began surfing before he could play a forward defence and his big shoulders and cut physique were almost solely attributable to hours of paddling through the surf in search of the perfect ride.

The combination of cricketing talent and an ingrained love of surfing and the beach made Cam Peters a sponsor's dream. The mental strength to prosper in a game where brain beats bicep and acceptance into the laid-back world of surf culture gave him the 'he's a legend but he's one of us' popularity that most sports stars can't bridge. His demeanour, coupled with his curly blond hair, deeply tanned skin and olive-green eyes, saw his image on everything from sunglasses to soft drinks. He had it all and he had the game to back it up.

56

Pilot Bay at Mt Maunganui has a special stillness, nestled as it is on the leeward side of an isthmus on the east cost of the North Island of New Zealand. Cam Peters enjoyed this stillness on a regular basis with the bay being just a few steps from his beachside apartment. Peters' early morning routine usually involved a surf, a trim latte and an iPad, with which he would flick through the pages of the New Zealand Herald, accompanied by the foreshore sounds of sea birds and a languid tide.

Of late, Peter's coffee and news update had been sullied by headlines of the deaths of many of the world's great cricketers. He thought about the contests he had enjoyed with these men. The dressing-room beers and the texted banter. It was difficult to conceive of the motive for removing such entertainers from the stage. Not all of them were best-mate material but the desire to finish them off and deprive the world of their talents was mystifying.

The ICC investigator, Mike Dunn, had told him to be as paranoid as he could be and that he would be down to New Zealand as soon as flight schedules would allow and certainly within a week. "Really good bugger, Abhi," Peters reflected as he contemplated the restrictions to his lifestyle Dunn had suggested. If a bloke like that isn't safe in Goa, then maybe Dunn had a point but it seemed a long way from the security-free life he was enjoying. Even at the peak of his fame, earache from an overzealous fan was about as dangerous as things got.

Peters had agreed to be part of a celebrity triathlon team in the coming weekend – news that had not thrilled Dunn but Peters was not a man to make a commitment and not honour it, particularly as the event was a major fund-raiser for the Cancer Council, a charity of special significance to the Peter's family. The loss of both his father and his uncle made the annual swim/bike/run a 'must-attend' whenever he was in the country.

Peters flipped the cover on his iPad and thought about his options for the day. Rounding up the boys for a net session seemed a good way to take care of an hour or two with the added benefit of the unfiltered advice from his mates about the whole 'World XI' situation. He could hear them now.

"Reckon a player of your talent would be pretty safe."

"Not a bad time to be twelthy." Although they admired him greatly, there was little chance that hubris or conceit would flourish in their company.

Popping his coffee cup in the recycling bin, Peter's thought another brew was in order before the day began properly. As he approached the café, he noticed a man out front tapping on his computer. *Oh God*, he thought, *not that prick – why would he be down at the Mount?* The second coffee now seemed as appealing as a Durian smoothie but as he pivoted to make his escape a voice confirmed his worst fears.

"Hi, Cam, not sure if you remember me – the name's Frank – Frank Mellem. I'm in town for a few days and wondered if I could do a feature on you. I have a feeling time is against us."

57

Gareth Wickramysinghe, a slightly built man with a wispy beard and head of hair that would make a barber withdraw his daily special sign had fashioned a remarkable career as a spin bowler for the Sri Lankan cricket team. Despite a pedigree which suggested academia – mother a geologist from Wales, (hence Gareth) and father an economics lecturer at the University of Ruhuna, Gareth found cricket at a young age. His studious and analytical nature lent itself perfectly to working out the weaknesses of his opposition and even at a young age he was attracting comparisons to the pantheon of spinners who had brought such esteem to Sri Lanka through their deeds on the cricket field. It surprised only his father when he was selected for Sri Lanka and in the ensuing years, he had collected wickets around the world but more particularly at his beloved home ground, the Galle International Stadium.

Normally, a proud man with a demeanour just on the pleasant side of arrogant, tonight he cowered in the Loft Suite at the Galle Fort Hotel. All of his 324 test scalps counted for nothing as he sat on the bed like a babysitter who couldn't remember if they'd locked the back door. Every noise was magnified, his sense of well-being not assisted by the wooden passageways that led to his room, nor the giggles and muttered conversations of guests as they made their way past his room and on to their evening arrangements. There was nothing to suggest he had made the murderer's team, although, not helpfully, the local media felt it would be an outrage if he missed out. It was more the call from the English investigator, Dunn, that had him so rattled.

"Gareth, it's Mike Dunn here."

"You've no doubt seen and heard what has been going on and, of course, most recently the death of Abhi Misra. We think the killer is either headed for Sri Lanka or New Zealand. And when I say Sri Lanka, I really mean he is headed for you. Now, we don't know that for sure but get yourself to the Galle Fort and ask for Chaminda John. Chaminda will make sure security is first class and he and his team will monitor all entrants to the hotel. Try to relax, Gareth. I'm on my way."

Well, that's great, Mike, he thought. *I'm sitting here like some form of live bait waiting for a psychopath to drop by and it's still a fifty-fifty that he's even going to come to Sri Lanka.*

He'd checked in a day ago, made himself known to Mr John and then had barely left the room. He contemplated room service but then recalled how Misra had been murdered. Best to give the mini bar the once over. Sadly, Pringles crisps, a Kit Kat and some designer liquorice were the only items resembling food but he dismissed his recently received dietary advice and made short work of all three, hoping their combined calories would see him through the night. The trill of the phone just about sent him into orbit and he clawed his way across the bedspread to pick up.

"Hello?"

"Gareth, it is Chaminda here. Everything OK?"

"Yes, fine, Chaminda, thank you. Look, there is no need to ring and check on me. If you've got all entrances covered, I'm happy to wait it out."

"OK, no problem. Mr Dunn will be here in the morning, so I'll get back in touch then."

"Fine, thank you. Oh, one thing, could you check the Wi-Fi password and text it to me? I never got around to watching *Narcos* and I get the feeling tonight could be a good one for a binge."

A text message buzzed through in due course and he made a little stand for his iPad using the mass of pillows which adorned the bed. *Things could be worse,* he thought as he made his way through the early years of Escobar's career. Four episodes in, he became drowsy and nodded off, letting his guard down for the first time since he checked in.

58

Lucinda Wright was on to her second Old-Fashioned by the time Subro Singhal made his way into the hotel bar. It hadn't been her intention to consult the cocktail list and had approached the bar with a view to enjoying a sparkling iced-water with a slice of lemon, despite the notoriety that particular combination had earned in recent times. As it happened, the sight of the barman mixing up for another customer, the large spherical piece of ice and the promise of a gentle burn at the back of her throat had her uttering, "Another one of those, please, but with whisky for me," in a tone just on the edge of desperate. The combination of the travel, the investigation and the heat had her resting the ice on her top lip and letting half the contents make a soothing swirl in her mouth.

Subro sat down next to her and handed her a file. It contained still shots of the alleged murderer at various points in the hotel, a copy of his bill and the registration of a Hertz rental vehicle he had left in the hotel car park. The name Ian Michael Heamana had been used for both the hotel and the car rental and it appeared he had attended a financial planning seminar at the hotel during his stay. On the surface, just another businessman enjoying a tax write-off at a resort but the presence of a waiter's uniform in his room and the coincidence of his appearance and physical disability left Lucinda in no doubt that this was their man – but was this man Martin Fowler and if so, why the alias? It wasn't as if they'd established anything, at least nothing he would have been aware of, so the whole fake I.D, false passport ruse was just another way of getting caught, particularly with the enhanced security for border crossings.

"OK, Subro, so where's our man now?"

"That is not known for certain but I've got Vinny checking the data logs from the hotel server. It might give us something."

Wright narrowly avoided a sigh of exasperation. "All right, give me a bit more, Subro. What is known for certain and where are the gaps?"

"We know that this Mr Heamana checked-out and that a chauffeur-driven limousine took him to the airport."

"Brilliant." Given the airport has been described variously as 'not a place to linger' and 'like going through hell', it was highly unlikely he'd be holed up in the airport lounge. "There must be a record of his departure."

Subro grimaced and dipped his head like a terrier that had been discovered nibbling on his master's Gucci loafers. "That would be a reasonable assumption, Ms Wright, but unfortunately, there is no record of a Mr Heamana leaving Goa. It would appear that his resourcefulness also includes access to a number of travel documents."

"Christ, Subro, you have got to be kidding me! This guy just vanishes like Keyser Soze and we're sitting here looking at old photos and car rental agreements. Our murderer could be anywhere by now. Tell me, where do the direct flights from Goa take you? There can't be that many destinations."

"There are 13 in India and a handful of international destinations, Ms Wright. I'm afraid that line of elimination is not likely to be particularly fruitful. You need to think about where he might end up rather than how he might get there."

Wright raised both palms by way of apology. "Thanks, Subro. Sorry, I'm a bit terse. We're having a frustrating time getting close to this guy. Look, I've got to check in with London and then I might think about a flight out tomorrow. By the looks of things, I think we might be done here."

"Very well, Ms Wright. Call me if you need anything and once you know your plans, I will arrange transport and ride with you to the airport. If you would excuse me."

"Very decent of you. I'll call you a little later on. Bye."

Although a third Old-Fashioned was becoming inevitable. She decided to ring Gordon and see if he had any updates. It was late afternoon in Goa, so with the time difference she knew Gordy would have been at it for a few hours already, even though it was just approaching mid-morning in London.

"Gordon Landolfi speaking."

"Gordon, it's Lu here. How are things your end?"

"No breakthroughs to speak of yet, Lu. I'll fill you in as soon as anything concrete comes to hand but what have you found in Goa?"

"To be frank, not a lot, I'm afraid. Our link to Mr Heamana is based on suspicion rather than hard evidence at this point but the appearance and the waiter's uniform draw a nice loop around him. The problem is, our Mr Heamana has scarpered but not as himself. It would appear he's one of those Jason Bourne types with three or four passports and a wad of notes in a dozen currencies."

"I'm getting from that we have no steer on his next destination?"

"Not from any airport intelligence. Our closest step would be the selection of his 'cricket team', which probably means Sri Lanka or New Zealand. Mike is en route to Galle as we speak. Let's hope he doesn't have to turn up with a body bag."

With no flights leaving until the following morning, Lucinda Wright decided that a third Old-Fashioned before dinner wouldn't hurt. In fact, in the interests of variety, perhaps a Negroni might be a better bet. Might as well sip away and enjoy the evening as it would soon be on the plane, back to the office and back into the grind.

The barman was just squeezing the essence from the orange peel when an excited Vineet Syam appeared beside her.

"Hello, Vineet, popping in for a drink?"

"No, no, Ms Wright, I have found something that you are certain to be intrigued by."

"Oh, really, Vineet? You have my attention, although I have to say the only thing I'm intrigued by at the moment is the flavour of this Negroni."

"Please, Ms Wright, put down your drink."

"Hey, steady on. If I want drinking advice, I've got a perfectly irritating mother-in-law to take care of that. What have you got for me?"

"Apologies, Ms Wright, but I am certain this is important. I made some searches through the hotel server. There is a program called Wireshark which enabled me to run through all the log file data."

"You'd better cut to the chase – you started to lose me at 'server'."

"Well, here is the intriguing bit. Mr Heamana made several searches during his time here. I don't know the correct pronunciation but he was looking for connecting flights and accommodation in a place in New Zealand. 'Mt Manganewy' is the name."

Lucinda grabbed his screen and looked at the search. Sure enough, several lines had 'Mt Maunganui' in the thread.

"Vineet, you are a genius. Can you tell if he's booked anywhere or is it just search results?"

"Unfortunately, we cannot determine where he intends to stay or how he intends to get there, only that it is rather obvious he is going there at some stage. As for when, who knows?"

59

Gareth Wickramysinghe went from a deep sleep to blind terror in the time it takes for the human ear to pick up the unmistakeable sound of a plastic key engaging the lock on a hotel room door.

He leapt to his feet and adopted what he hoped looked like a martial arts pose but realised that his bony frame and baggy boxer shorts made him look more Tommy Lee than Bruce Lee. Realising a physical confrontation was a losing prospect, he decided a threatening voice might detract the visitor from entering but the tension that gripped his body turned his 'Who is it?' into a sound more reminiscent of a cat dealing with a stubborn hairball. He grabbed the iron from the bench and raised it in readiness. The intruder took a step inside and adopted a defensive pose at the sight of the raised iron.

"Gareth, it's me. I've been wanting to see you for some time. So pleased I could track you down."

The only redeeming feature of the voice was that it was female and Dunn had told him that the person they felt was committing the murders was undoubtedly male.

"Charuta, is that you? Christ, woman, you nearly scared me to death!"

"Yes, it's me, Gareth. Why have you been avoiding me?"

"I'm sorry, Charuta, we can get to that but how the hell did you get past security – and what are you even doing here?"

"Everyone knows I'm your girlfriend. They agreed you could use the company."

"Charuta, you were my girlfriend but when you announced to anyone within earshot at the Tap House that you hoped I would die slowly in pain and that you never wanted see my scrawny arse again, I assumed I was free to do whatever the hell I wanted from there. I haven't seen or heard from you in over a month and you just flash a smile at security and wander into my room? Do you know why I'm even here?"

"Not really. I heard something about some cricketers being killed but what does that have to do with you?"

"The head of the investigation thinks I am the likely next target, so suggested I hole up here because the 'security is so good' – no match for you though, so I'm thinking a serial killer might not find it too demanding either. Charuta, you need to leave now and get Chaminda John to call me straight away."

"It's three o'clock in the morning, are you sure that's what you want?" she asked with a suggestive grin and a raised eyebrow. "C'mon, baby."

"C'mon, baby? Really? Goodnight, Charuta. Thanks for stopping by but I need to get this security worked out. I'm sure the concierge can get a taxi arranged for you."

The door had no sooner clicked shut than he lay back down on the bed, preparing a barrage for the head of security. *Come on, Mr Dunn,* he thought. *These guys are gonna get me killed.*

60

Gordon Landolfi didn't really enjoy googling and in fact was mildly annoyed that it had even become a verb. Myriad searches for Marty Fowler and various derivations of same were starting to bring diminishing returns for the effort and late hours being put into the work. Deciding that 'Fowler' as a search word might have run its course, He went back to his police work basics and started searching for every connection that Marty Fowler might have had from young sportsman to stockbroker to latent Indian tourist.

None of the names from the New Zealand team at the youth tournament brought anyone of fame and Landolfi smiled ruefully at how the promise and imagined futures of such players must have caused such pride in their respective families. A decade or so later and some of them are pulling pints or working office jobs, their once athletic bodies sporting the evidence of Friday night drinks and the morning tea run. Landolfi's thoughts moved to Fowler's injury and the rugby team (what was he thinking playing rugby?) and as he scrolled through the list of players, the name Justin Ilesman stood out as the only deceased member of the team. Curiosity piqued, a couple more entries and a couple of clicks and up came the story of the young man who had tragically fallen from the cliffs above St Heliers Bay. The fall was described as mystifying but with no evidence of 'foul play', the coroner was content to file it as a tragic accident, a decision Landolfi found a touch convenient and probably the result of lazy police work.

Landolfi figured the next significant move in Fowler's life was having his knee ruined and then repaired, so he worked his way through Auckland surgeons, Auckland orthopaedic specialists and then bingo, a gentleman by the name of Max LaFarge appeared on the search results page. While the other practitioners were there as a means of contact, Mr LaFarge appeared as a result of his untimely demise. In this case, a few suspects were brought in – his wife, his wife's lover and a string of unhappy customers. The former patients were brought in largely because of the brutal nature of his murder – a neatly cut throat was one thing but to shred the anterior cruciate ligament on both knees seemed a little over the top, particularly as the forensic team had determined that the knees followed the throat by some time. Among the ex-patients was the former New Zealand youth team cricketer, Marty Fowler. This is getting a tad interesting thought, Landolfi, and although it was past ten in the evening, he was determined to help deliver on Mike Dunn's hunch. It wasn't that he had anything that would interest a judge but Fowler was connected to people who had died both prematurely and violently. He hopped back to the search results from the rugby team and saw a couple of links to players through the websites of their current employers. Finding one who worked in sports marketing and checking that it was a reasonable hour in New Zealand, he dialled the firm's number.

"Global Sports, this is Brenda speaking."

"Hi, Brenda, I was hoping to speak to Steve Evans, please."

"Putting you through now."

"Steve Evans, can I help?"

"Hi, Steve, my name is Gordon Landolfi and I'm with the ICC. I'm investigating a case and wondered if you could help me with some background?"

"I'm happy to help if I can, Gordon. I'm assuming it's cricket related?"

"Not exactly, Steve, it's more about your time in your school first XV. I wanted to ask you about Marty Fowler."

"Geez, that was a while ago and I haven't seen Marty for ages. He was never really one of the rugby guys. You may know he was a star cricketer and was just playing a bit of rugby between seasons."

"Yes, I read he was a gun cricketer but apparently, an accident put a stop to all that. Can you tell me what happened?"

"Yeah, we were playing around in the gym because the fields had been closed due to the lousy weather we had in Auckland that winter. We'd done a bit of fitness and were winding down with a bit of indoor soccer – that's when it happened."

"Tell me what happened, Steve."

"Marty had possession and being Marty just wanted to score himself, so getting a pass was out of the question. Then one of the guys just clobbered him from the side. There's not a bloke who was there that doesn't still grimace at the sound of the knee collapsing."

"So, who was the guy that slid in? He must feel terrible."

"Actually, he doesn't feel much about anything now. The guy who did it checked out a year or two back."

Landolfi felt an eerie wave ride up his back. "I'm picking the guy who did the clobbering was Justin Ilesman, the same one who fell off a cliff a year or so back?"

"The same. What's this all about?"

"Just covering off a few angles. Thanks, Steve, you've been very helpful."

Landolfi put down the receiver and let out a long whistle.

61

When Dunn landed in Colombo. His phone pinged and jangled like he'd just picked up the jackpot on the fruit machine at the Ring of Bells. Scrolling through the various messages, it was the bold type in capitals with the red exclamation mark which caught his eye in among reminders from his dentist, a special offer from John Lewis and an invitation from his mate Roger to a barbecue in Fulham. Sorry, Rog, that one might have to wait.

Lucinda Wright's message was clear. "He might be going to Sri Lanka but he is definitely going to New Zealand. Ask Cam Peters if he is going to be in Mt Maunganui this weekend."

Dunn was a picture of jaded frustration as he cleared customs and collected his luggage. Unfortunately, the call from Wright came too late for him to transit on and he still might have to check in on Wickramysinghe, so he trudged into arrivals, grabbed a coffee and rang Lucinda Wright.

"Morning, Lu, how are you today? Assume you are still in Goa?"

"Hi, Mike, I'm fine and yes, I'm still in Goa. I leave for the airport in about an hour."

"Tell me more about this lead in New Zealand."

"One of the investigative team here was particularly gifted when it came to technology and digital footprints. He managed to go through the hotel data and discovered an inordinate amount of material looking at New Zealand and Mt Maunganui in particular. Isn't that where Cam Peters lives?"

"I believe so and your message is spot on. I'll check to see if he is there this weekend. Knowing our killer, that information is probably already public. He doesn't appear to do much on the off-chance."

"Mike, it's potentially a big call but if Wickramysinghe is off-limits in Galle, why don't you just head for New Zealand?"

"I think you're right. I'll call Gareth and his security detail to see if there has been anything untoward happen but if he is locked up and safe, we're better to try and put a ring around Cam Peters. Nice bit of work that, Lu."

"Well, it was more young, Vineet, but thanks. We might finally be getting ahead of this guy. I'm going to get back to London. I'll check in once I've had time to catch up with Gordy."

Dunn drained the last of what was a pretty average double-shot cappuccino and despite the quality, he opted to reload and this time acquiesced to the advice of the assistant who convinced him it really did make more sense to take the sandwich deal. A second moderate coffee was accompanied by a ham and cheese sandwich that was showing its age. Hunger trumped nutritional value with ease and he munched it down in two bites while dialling the sequestered spinner.

"Gareth speaking."

"Gareth, it's Mike Dunn. How are you?"

"Mike, when are you getting here? Tell me you have landed in Sri Lanka?"

"I have Gareth but I need to talk to you about arrangements from here. Tell me, do you feel you are secure there?"

"I did until an ex-girlfriend made her way past security at three o'clock this morning. It's bloody ridiculous," replied Wickramysinghe in a voice which betrayed as much fear as it did anger.

"Good grief, that wasn't in the brief. I had every faith in Chaminda John. Have you spoken to him?"

"I did but I must confess my stress meant I may have been a little rude. The sledges from the Australians on the recent tour there broadened my ability to be abusive in English and we haven't spoken since. Perhaps you might be able to intercede and get things back on track? If he walks off the job, I'm pretty much cannon-fodder."

Dunn grinned to himself at the Sri Lankan's quaint expression. "OK, I'll do that, Gareth. The thing is, I'm considering heading straight to New Zealand as we have a strong lead suggesting our killer has passed you by."

"That's good to hear and I hope you're right. I'll stay right here, just, please, patch things up with Chaminda."

"I'll give him a call now – he'll be fine. If I get any more information about our killer's whereabouts, I relay it back through him. Enjoy the downtime, Gareth."

Dunn clicked off and immediately phoned Priscilla in the London office.

"Hi, P, it's Mike. I need to get to New Zealand, as soon as you can make it happen. I'll probably have to get to Singapore or Hong Kong and connect through one of those. Just whatever gets me out of here and down to Auckland the fastest."

"From Colombo? On it, Mike. I'll email details once confirmed. Anything else?"

"Yes, if you could put me through to Gordy, that would be great. Thanks, P."

"Mike, how are you, sir!"

"Good, Gordy, but I could have done without a trip to Colombo for no reason. What have you got for me?"

"It seems our man got a taste for killing some time ago. If the pieces fit together, and it certainly looks that way, I think there's a case to answer for two murders in Auckland a few years back, before he even started on his World XI spree."

"And you're convinced it's this Marty Fowler character?"

"Looks that way. Hey, I got that note from Lucinda. Sounds like NZ is the place to be right now."

"Yeah, Gordy, but for all the wrong reasons. I'm heading there as soon as P can organise flights. I'll be in touch."

62

As the killer made his way across the Indian Ocean, he reflected on his work to date. The comparative ease with which he had built his 'World XI' surprised him, despite his meticulous planning and the propensity for low paid workers around the world to be compromised for a week's wages. His knowledge of cricketers' habits and their public schedules was a key factor in his success but some of the finer details certainly needed more than just a bribe and a 'look the other way'.

The killer knew the invincibility and infallibility these men felt – it was as he had felt during the World Age Group tournament years before. Poised for a life of riches and public profile, the thought of someone wanting to murder him would have been laughable – we are heroes and more like to be suffocated by adulation than feel the sharp end of an assassin's knife. Of course, the injury meant he could only imagine what they all thought but he was close enough to it to 'know' and this was the foundation of his bitterness, the fuel for his rage.

How he loved the attention and servitude – this would have been my life, he reflected as the attendant proffered a significant measure of scotch. One or two more of those and a couple of Temazepam and I'll be in Hong Kong before I know it. A couple of nights there and I'll be set up for the final task – back home to deal with the man I was destined to be.

As the plane dipped into Chep Lap Lok, the attendant brushed the killer's shoulder.

"Sir, I must insist that you return your seat to the upright position, we are ready to land in Hong Kong."

"Yes, no problem – my apologies, got into a deep sleep there."

His passage around the world was the riskiest part of this process and without some inside help, he knew that this was where the entire plan could come unstuck. As they cruised down the runway looking for a gate, he grabbed his phone and dialled his contact. Checking in before immigration had been crucial at each step and thus far his passage had been seamless. As an international

202

number, it took some time to find a dial tone but before long he could tell the recipient would be hearing the chirping of his phone.

The phone was answered in a curt and clipped manner.

"Guy Trinnick speaking."

63

Dunn was baffled. The various sightings of the killer, although brief and relying on memory, had allowed for a solid identikit resemblance to be constructed. Footage had shown a man resembling the image entering Hong Kong and then boarding a flight to New Zealand, completely unencumbered by immigration officials at any of the passport-control checkpoints along the way.

What the hell was Trinnick doing? he wondered, as this was page one stuff in terms of picking up criminals.

Not only was Dunn baffled, he was also beyond exhausted. A flight to Hong Kong from Colombo and then the Hong Kong Airways red-eye had him landing in Auckland in the early hours local time. The imminent threat to Peter's life had induced support from the local police and Dunn was relieved to have Detective Constable Byron Fitzpatrick to accompany him on the two-and-a-half-hour drive to Mt Maunganui. Fitzpatrick had been a handy club footballer in his day and bore the indiscriminate scars that a few seasons of senior rugby in Auckland will inevitably deliver. Despite an exterior that suggested membership of 'Fight Club', Fitzpatrick was an astute policeman with several well-earned convictions to his name.

Surprisingly for one of such pedigree, Fitzpatrick loved to chat and was quick to draw Dunn into conversation about the case.

"When did you reckon this was about picking a cricket team?"

"It was quite early on, just after Andy Beaumont was killed. It was just a hunch then but we were on the money."

"So how come all these players haven't been quarantined, Mike? Given the ICC rankings, it wouldn't be too hard to work out who was in his sights."

"Fair point but most of these guys have strong public profiles and have people around them most of the time. We've urged the players to be careful but it would be overkill to drum up some witness protection program for them all."

He regretted his choice of words but if Fitzpatrick had picked up on it, he didn't let on.

"OK," replied Byron. "I get that. So what makes you so certain that Cam Peters is under threat?"

"We know that a man matching the closest thing we have to the killer's appearance came through Auckland Airport two days ago. No offence to you Kiwis, but Cam would be the only cricketer worthy of selection, given the rankings."

A period of silence fell over the car and as Highway 27 approached Matamata, Dunn asked Fitzpatrick if they could find a coffee somewhere soon.

"No worries, Mike. Workmans is a good spot, might grab a couple of club sarnies to get us over the Kaimais too, eh?"

Dunn was a little uncertain about Fitzpatrick's meaning but gave a quick "Yeah, why not". Coffee had become Dunn's constant companion over the investigation and he was intrigued to find out what a small town (albeit one famous for Hobbits) could deliver.

As they waited for the coffee – long black for Dunn, trim latte for Fitzpatrick – Dunn enquired as to the security on offer at the race event unfolding in Mt Maunganui.

"Gee, Mike, not the best, eh?" replied Fitzpatrick.

"When you say 'not the best' what am I to take from that?"

"Apart from a few cops blocking some of the roads, it's pretty much a free-for-all – there's 30 odd k's of houses, spectators and beachfront. All they try and do is make it a clear path for the competitors and that's about it. We've got a couple of guys with eyes on the turnaround area but I've seen better security at a Wiggles concert."

Bloody brilliant, thought Dunn, not entirely sure who the Wiggles were but pretty sure it meant 'sod all'.

"OK, we're going to have to get close to Cam. How are you on a bike, Byron?"

"Didn't pack my lycra, Mike, but I'll give it a crack," he said with a grin as Dunn's hope for at least one sentence that didn't contain local vernacular evaporated.

64

The day had dawned as any other would during the Bay of Plenty summer. A cool breeze complemented the early sunshine, the sky an opaque blue, the water its mirror. Hundreds of athletes were doing what athletes do – stretching, visualising, tweaking and swapping handshakes of goodwill and support. For most, a triathlon is a contest with oneself, so the pre-race atmosphere is about common bonds, brother and sisterhood – no trash talk, no mind games, just encouragement and support for the challenge ahead.

Cam Peters looked around in awe as the competitors got suited up and ready for the plunge into Pilot Bay. He thought himself fit but these men and women gave lean a new dimension. Peters was not doing the long version of the triathlon but rather a truncated version specifically designed so that celebrities of modest aerobic capacity could still compete, draw a crowd and help with the fundraising effort. Many were doing just one of the three legs but Peters saw this as a great way to keep the fitness on point so put up his hand for all the cut-down event, a 1 km swim, 20 km bike and 10 km run. Although cool at race start, Peters knew that by late morning, the late spring temperatures would in the mid-20s – not a good time to be slogging it out with the battlers.

From a balcony in one of the tower blocks on Marine Parade, the killer ran his sight over the melee of neoprene and fluoro swimming caps. How marvellous that every competitor was so clearly identified with race numbers prominently displayed for officials and spectators alike. Adding to the simplicity of the killer's task was the staggered start which further broke the density of this concentration of triceps and finely sculpted calf muscles. Cam Peter's group was called to the start line – Peters, a couple of Super Rugby players, a breakfast DJ from Wellington and the captain of the New Zealand netball team were the only ones who could claim recognition beyond the region, while the rest of the group were 'local personalities', a kind of second-string rent-a-crowd. As the high fives and 'go hard bro's' rippled through the group, the killer twisted the dial to sharpen the image. His view of Peters was now relatively unimpeded and he could take in his physical characteristics as if they were standing in a bar together.

The competitors approached the starting line and crouched, ready for the short burst down the sand and the leap into Pilot Bay's coolish waters.

The gun shot caught many by surprise with many spectators adopting a protective crouch at its report. Peters began to pitch forward as if held up only by the adhesion of the soft sand but soon found his stride and within seconds was leaping over the first breaker. The starter's gun had startled many, the sound being out of tune with a glorious Mt Maunganui morning. Momentary disorientation over, the crowd began to yell their encouragement and as more streams of competitors entered the sea, a frothy effervescence covered the field. The killer had eyes for Peters and Peters alone – his plan required detailed knowledge of Peters' passage through the course and although he would lose sight of him from time to time during the race, the more he knew, the more his margin for missed opportunity was reduced. He had decided not to plan a strike during the bike leg but his idea for the run seemed an absolute certainty – a tired Peters would be unaware and with surprise on his side, it would be his easiest murder yet.

65

The killer had moved casually around the base track and now sat among the grass on the northern slopes of Mt Maunganui. On another day, in another mind-set, this would be the perfect place for a glass of Chardonnay and a picnic with a pretty woman but today, it was the perfect place for a murder. Dressed in Nike runners, Under Armour shorts and a Penrith Panthers training shirt, he was just another bloke among the foliage, enjoying the sun and yelling the odd word of encouragement to the passing runners.

Spectators were few on the side of the mountain and the killer had found a spot that suited his needs perfectly. Nestled beside a Pohutukawa tree, he was a short drop to the track, which was less than two metres across. In contrast to the safety of the bank, the seaward side offered no protection at all and a misstep would result in a 15-metre fall to the oyster-clad rocks below, before an inevitable roll into the tidal swells that shaped the cliffs. A short slide, a solid shove and Cam Peters would join his 11.

Cam Peters had made the changeover point after completing the bike leg in good time. Taking some time to dry his feet and don his Asics, he was looking forward to the run ahead. It was mid-morning – the sun was warm but not oppressive and the sea breeze offered a natural coolant for the ten kilometres ahead. Two laps of the base track and a couple of lengths of Marine Parade and he'd be enjoying a Steinlager and swapping stories with his charity team. The thought of getting to know the national netball captain better put a little extra bounce in his stride as he headed down The Mall, toward the base of the Mount.

Dunn found a park in Bank St, adjacent to the marshalling area. Progress had been slow over the mountain range which skirts the Bay of Plenty and Fitzpatrick was sure they had missed the bike leg.

"How can we tell where Peters is?" asked Dunn, his voice a mixture of anxiety, exasperation and straight-out fatigue.